WHAT CAME FROM THE STARS

WHAT CAME FROM THE STARS

Gary D. Schmidt

CLARION BOOKS

Houghton Mifflin Harcourt

Boston | New York | 2012

Clarion Books
215 Park Avenue South
New York, New York 10003

Clarion Books is an imprint of
Houghton Mifflin Harcourt Publishing Company.

www.hmhbooks.com

The text was set in Sabon Roman and italic.
Map illustration by Blake Henry
Design by Christine Kettner

LIBRARY OF CONGRESS CATALOGING-IN-PUBLICATION DATA

Schmidt, Gary D.
What came from the stars / by Gary D. Schmidt.

p. cm.

Summary: In a desperate attempt for survival, a peaceful
civilization on a faraway planet besieged by a dark lord
sends its most precious gift across the cosmos into the
lunch box of Tommy Pepper, sixth-grader, of Plymouth,
Massachusetts.

ISBN 978-0-547-61213-3 (hardcover)

[1. Fantasy. 2. Plymouth (Mass.)—Fiction.] I. Title.
PZ7.S3527Wh 2012

[Fic]—dc23
2011045439

Manufactured in the United States of America
DOC 10 9 8 7 6 5 4 3 2 1
4500370914

For James,
with your father's dear love

Contents

1. The Last Days of the Valorim | 1

2. Tommy Pepper's Birthday | 8

3. The Wrath of the Lord Mondus | 30

4. Yellow Flags | 35

5. The Treachery of the Faithless Valorim | 56

6. Tommy Pepper's Mother | 61

7. The Woe of the Ethelim | 83

8. Storms | 88

9. A Journey Across the Dark | 111

10. The Plymouth Fall Festival | 116

11. Hileath | 138

12. The Fah Smell of Seaweed | 143

13. Uprising | 165

14. Mr. PilgrimWay | 170

15. Battle at the Reced | 192

16. Storms Again | 197

17. The Journey of Ealgar, Who Would Be Called the Bold | 217

18. The O'Mondim | 222

19. The Last Battle of Young Waeglim | 248

20. What Was Lost and What Was Found | 252

21. The New Days of the Ethelim | 274

   The Testament of Young Waeglim | 279

   A List of Weird and Strange Words . . . | 288

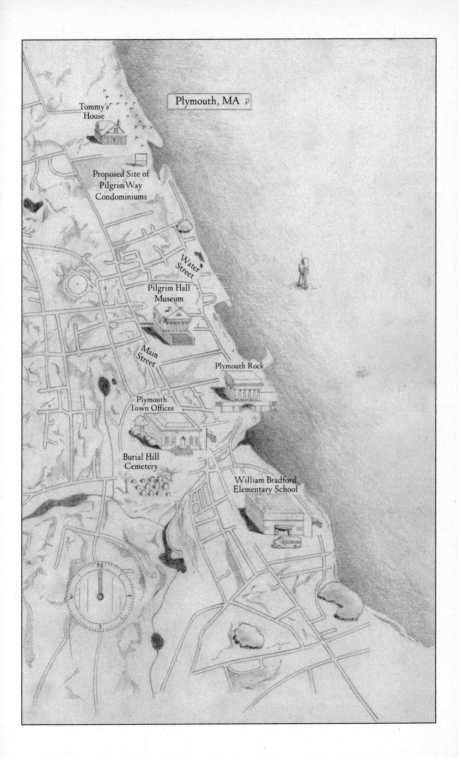

ONE

The Last Days of the Valorim

So the Valorim came to know that their last days were upon them. The Reced was doomed, and the Ethelim they had loved well and guarded long would fall under the sharp trunco of the faceless O'Mondim and the traitors who led them. The Valorim looked down from the high walls of the Reced and knew they would find no mercy in the dark fury of the O'Mondim massed below—none for all they had loved.

Not a one of the Valorim did not weep for what would be lost forever.

Not a one of the Ethelim did not fear what would come.

But the Valorim would not yield, though day after day they watched the O'Mondim flash the gray metal of their trunco, though day after day they heard the O'Mondim pound at the barricaded gates of the

Reced. But a First Sunrise finally came when the hearts of the Valorim began to beat with the rhythm of the battering rams, and by Second Sunrise, the gates could hold no more. The Valorim abandoned the Outer Court and fled into the Great Hall of the Reced, where the hanoraho had once sounded for the victories of the Valorim, and where there was none now left to play them. They barred the doors, and in the Great Hall, the sons of Brythelaf stayed with orluo drawn and held before them.

The Valorim fell back into the inner courts, and then upward into the Council Room of the Ethelim, which held the Twelve Seats of the Reced. There did the ten daughters of Hild stand, while the last Elders of the Valorim were brought into the Tower, and the stout doors of the Tower closed and barricaded behind them—though none believed those doors would hold the tide of the faceless O'Mondim.

And truly, when the O'Mondim found the Great Hall closed, their fury was renewed, and the last Elders heard the battering of the iron rams at the doors of the Great Hall, and the terrible groaning of the O'Mondim.

Then spoke Ecthael, who had warned to no avail of the treachery of the Lord Mondus and the stirrings of the O'Mondim.

"Now are the days of rancor ended. Now is the time of feuding over. Only these few remain of the Faithful Valorim, and when we have passed, who will stand by the Ethelim then? Who will guard the Twelve Seats? First Sunrise saw the blood of the O'Mondim spilled over the Reced steps, but Second Sunset will see our own. The Song is over. The Silence begins."

Then spoke Brythelaf. He spoke words of anger. "Ever have you warned of the Silence," he said. "Ever have you spoken of unending woe." He faced the other Valorim. "I say this: It may be that our time is over. Perhaps the Silence that we beat back with the strength of our hearts at Brogum Sorg Cynna—there were gumena weardas!—perhaps that Silence may overwhelm us and the Ethelim we guard. It may be. But if it is to be, then let us take all our song, our story, our beloit, gliteloit, all we have made from our hearts, all we have brought against the Silence, and let us forge it together and send it out from us, so that the Art of the Valorim might still be heard and seen and known even when the Valorim are no longer. Then shall the Silence be defeated."

A great cheer rose from the Valorim in the Tower, and from the ten daughters of Hild in the Council Room of the Ethelim, and from the sons of Brythelaf in the Great Hall, and the sound of it chilled the hearts of the O'Mondim, so that for a moment their long arms weakened, and the rams battering at the doors of the Great Hall faltered. But for a moment only—and then, terrible was the strength of the O'Mondim.

So the Forge was heated again, as it had been long ago, heated in the uppermost of the Tower chambers, and one by one the Valorim Elders gave the songs of their hearts, and Young Waeglim shaped a Chain, green and silver, each link a piece of their Art, each link a piece of the Heart of the Valorim.

His striking hammer sounded even as the doors of the Great Hall were broken and the O'Mondim leaped through. Fierce were the sons of Brythelaf waiting for them there, and fierce their vengeance upon the O'Mondim. But the O'Mondim were more than could be counted.

Young Waeglim's hammer sounded even as the O'Mondim beat past the inner courts and upward into the Council Room of the Ethelim and beyond the Twelve Seats, where the ten daughters of Hild cleaved many before they too fell and the O'Mondim moved upward again.

Young Waeglim's hammer sounded even as the Tower door was breached, and the Valorim Elders, unto Ecthael, gave themselves now from chamber to chamber, from staircase to staircase, so that Young Waeglim's hammer might not be stilled. But the Valorim were hewn down one by one, and the faceless O'Mondim came to the uppermost of the Tower chambers, where the last two of the Valorim held. There the O'Mondim battered and smashed against that door until the framing splintered.

Then it was Brythelaf who stood in the doorway against the great and terrible host of the O'Mondim, his orlu before him. And it was Young Waeglim who stayed at the Forge, heating the last of the Art of the Valorim into the Chain. Grievous was the battle at the doorway, and grievous the wounds of the noble Brythelaf. But he would not yield, and he would not yield, not until Young Waeglim plucked the Chain of the Valorim Art from the fire of the Forge and carried it to the window of the Tower of the Reced. There he cupped the heated Chain to his chest, and when the Art of the Valorim beat with the song of his own heart, he held it out into the last dark light of setting Hengest, and on the breath of Young Waeglim's own Song and Thought, the Chain lifted away from him, higher, then higher, until it was so high that Young Waeglim could see its bright shining no more, and the Art of the Valorim flew from him and was gone.

Then did Brythelaf fall, and Young Waeglim did turn to meet the O'Mondim triumphant.

But the Chain of the Valorim Art flew upward, far away from the victory of the O'Mondim, and far from their sudden despair and fierce anger at the loss of what above all things the Lord Mondus had desired to hold in his hand, and for which he had hazarded all.

And so Second Sunset fell over the Ethelim, and their Reced, and their world.

But the Chain left that world, and the Song and Thought of Young Waeglim and the Art within that Chain gave it power. It flew past the highest clouds, through the blue air, and into the dark of cold and black space. It flew past moons and planets, past stars whose songs the Valorim had learned and sung, beyond the constellations that wheeled over their world and whose stories the Valorim had told the Ethelim. The Chain flew past comets and nebulae, and past more stars, strange constellations, and so, finally, out of the galaxy of that world.

And still it flew on through the cold darkness, past farther galaxies that had once shone to the Valorim like distant stars, and which the Chain tumbled by until it left those galaxies as small as single stars again. And so through cold light and colder darkness and cold light and colder darkness, the Chain sped.

And sped.

And sped, until listen! It came to a small wheeling galaxy, and to a single small star at the edge of that galaxy, and to a single small planet—blue like its own—that rolled around that star. The Chain streaked past its moon and shuddered into its canopy, where it fell, glittering in the light of the strange, single sun. It fell, passing through the cold mist of high white clouds, down through their shadows and into the sunlight again. It fell, cooling as it went, down toward the sea and the *green land and the red brick building, until, with a final tumble, the Chain of the Valorim Art, the Chain that held their Song, the Chain that was all that was left against the Silence, struck a window ledge, dangled through, skidded across a white plastic table top, fell toward a gray plastic bench, and dropped into the Ace Robotroid Adventure lunch box of Tommy Pepper, sixth-grader, of the class of Mr. Burroughs, of William Bradford Elementary School, of Plymouth, Massachusetts.*

It took some time before Tommy noticed.

TWO

Tommy Pepper's Birthday

It was Tommy Pepper's twelfth birthday, and for it he had unwrapped the dumbest birthday present in the history of the entire universe: an Ace Robotroid Adventure lunch box. On the top, Ace Robotroid was flying with the Robotroid Cosmic Flag in his hand. It billowed out over his cape, and an *R* for "Robotroid" glittered and shimmered depending on which way you held the lunch box. Inside, stamped on the cover, was a close-up of Ace Robotroid, who reminded him that "Even Though Robotroids Can't Drink Milk, Kids *Can* and *Should!*" Ace Robotroid held up one finger and smiled to help make the point.

The dumbest birthday present in the history of the entire universe.

Tommy Pepper hadn't watched *The Robotroids* since he was nine. Well, twice when he was ten. Maybe three times. But no more than three times that entire year. He looked around the cafeteria. If there was anyone else who had an Ace Robotroid Adventure lunch box like his, he was hiding it—the way Tommy was trying to hide his.

Or maybe, if someone else had one, he was accidentally losing it, which had been Tommy's plan as soon as he laid eyes on the thing, until his father—who had probably figured out Tommy's plan as soon as he laid eyes on the thing too—said, "Your grandmother always gives thoughtful presents. She probably waited in a very long line to get one of these."

Tommy had nodded.

"And you know, it's not easy for her to wait in a line anymore. She's getting older."

Tommy nodded again.

"And she sent it all the way from San Francisco."

"I know," said Tommy.

"And it was expensive."

Tommy sighed. If she had asked, he would have saved his grandmother the expense. A football. An authentic Tom Brady–signed football. That would have been worth waiting in line for.

"And it's not like she can afford to throw away . . ."

"All right," said Tommy. "I love it. I'm going to show it to every one of my friends and they'll wish they had one too. Pretty soon there's going to be all these grandmothers lined up to buy Ace Robotroid Adventure lunch boxes.

They'll be beating each other with canes to get the last one. Blood will be spilled! Lives will be imperiled! Here!" He held it out. "You better put this someplace safe!"

His father made Tommy take the dumb lunch box to school that morning. He packed in it a hard-boiled egg wrapped in a napkin, a plastic bag of celery and carrot sticks, a chicken salad sandwich on wheat with only a little mayonnaise, two raisin cookies, and—because not everything has to be as healthy as all get-out—a small carton of chocolate milk. He packed the same lunch for Patty, except she got strawberry milk. She liked the color.

When his father was done, Tommy put on his winter coat even though it was only September and still so warm that the trees hadn't even begun to blush.

"Are you cold?" said his father.

"I think there might be snow in the air," said Tommy.

His father handed them the lunch boxes.

As soon as they got out the door, Tommy hid the lunch box beneath his coat. ("Never mind," he said to his sister.) He hid it there all the way to school, and when he got to the sixth grade hall outside Mr. Burroughs's classroom, he took off his coat, wrapped it around the Ace Robotroid Adventure lunch box, and stuffed both of them into his locker.

Alice Winslow saw him doing this. "Why are you wearing a coat that's made for fall in Alaska?" she said.

"I'm not wearing a coat that's made for fall in Alaska," Tommy said.

"Do you think it's going to snow?"

"Stranger things have happened," said Tommy Pepper. He wiped the sweat from his face. "Cold fronts come in all the time. It starts to snow and people who only wore jackets because they thought it was still fall get caught in a blizzard and they die and then they're found in some snowbank, all blue and stiff. You never know. You should be prepared."

He closed his locker and twirled the combination lock.

"I really hope you're getting the help you need," said Alice Winslow.

Tommy Pepper ignored her.

But he worried about the Ace Robotroid Adventure lunch box all through the morning. Maybe he could dump his lunch out by his locker and carry the chocolate milk and the chicken salad sandwich to the cafeteria. Or, if anyone was too close, he could just take out the chocolate milk.

But that kind of plan never works. When the lunch bell rang, Tommy Pepper went to his locker and held the door mostly closed while he reached through his winter coat, found the Ace Robotroid Adventure lunch box, started to open it—and suddenly there was Mr. Burroughs, as if he had appeared out of subspace. "You've only got twenty minutes, Tommy," he said. "No time to pick and choose. Take the whole lunch box and let's go." He stood, waiting.

What could he do? Tommy took the Ace Robotroid Adventure lunch box and carried it to the cafeteria. He sat down close to the window and set it open on the gray plastic bench between himself and the wall. He breathed heavily. He thought he would give just about anything if only he could get the lunch box back into the locker without anyone seeing it. If he didn't—if anyone saw it—he was doomed.

When Patrick Belknap came and sat next to him, Tommy Pepper pushed the Ace Robotroid Adventure lunch box a little farther under the table while Patrick took out his own lunch. It was in a brown paper bag, which is what all lunches for sixth-graders should be in. How come only Tommy Pepper's father didn't get this?

When James Sullivan came and sat next to Patrick Belknap, Tommy Pepper pushed the Ace Robotroid Adventure lunch box to the very edge of the bench, as far under the table as it could get without some sort of antigravity device. James Sullivan laid his football—his authentic Tom Brady–signed football—on the table, and he put his lunch next to it. His lunch that was in a brown paper bag. Of course.

When Alice Winslow came and sat across from him and asked, "Were you wearing that coat because you were trying to hide something?" Tommy Pepper pushed the Ace Robotroid Adventure lunch box a little farther under the table again.

"No," he said.

"Hey, Pepper," said James Sullivan, "Mr. Burroughs said it was your birthday today. Is it your birthday?"

Tommy Pepper nodded. The Ace Robotroid Adventure lunch box teetered.

"So we get ice cream cake when we get back," said James Sullivan.

"And I get to play my . . ."

"Accordion," they all said.

"Accordion," said Patrick Belknap.

"We can hardly wait," said James Sullivan. "What did you get, Pepper?"

Tommy shrugged.

"Are you sure you weren't hiding something?" said Alice Winslow.

At the very end of the bench, Jeremy Hereford sat down. He was the smallest kid in the sixth grade. He weighed about what a cantaloupe weighs. Maybe it was the vibration of Jeremy's butt hitting the seat. Or maybe it had something to do with the quick flash of light Tommy saw at the window. But whatever it was, the Ace

Robotroid Adventure lunch box tipped enough, just enough, so that it fell down, down, and clattered its tinny clatter on the wood floor.

"What was that?" said Alice Winslow.

Tommy Pepper closed his eyes.

"What kind of ice cream do you think it will be this time?" said Patrick Belknap.

"Did something fall?" said Alice Winslow.

"Butter pecan," said James Sullivan.

"What fell?" said Alice Winslow.

"Probably his birthday present," said Patrick Belknap.

This is what happens when you are doomed, Tommy thought. It's all been decided. Nothing can stop it. Even your friends become part of the Universe's Plan of Doom and Destruction.

Tommy Pepper looked down beneath the cafeteria table at his fallen Ace Robotroid Adventure lunch box, and there among the spilled carrot and celery sticks, something . . . well, something glowed. Tommy blinked. Whatever it was, it really was glowing a little bit. He reached down and picked it up.

A chain. Green and silver. Heavy.

"Is that your present?" said Patrick Belknap.

Tommy nodded. He held the chain in the light.

"What a dumb present," said James Sullivan.

If you only knew, thought Tommy Pepper.

The chain wasn't glowing now. Maybe it only glowed in the dark. But even without the glowing, Tommy had never seen anything like it before. It seemed like there were four, or five, or six metal strands that wove around themselves, and sometimes a whole strand looked green, and sometimes a whole strand looked silver, and sometimes it all seemed to be changing from green to silver and back to green again.

"It's not dumb," said Alice Winslow. "It's beautiful."

"He got a beautiful chain for his birthday and you don't think that's dumb?"

"I got an accordion for my birthday," said Patrick Belknap.

"Don't need to say anything else, do I?" said James Sullivan. He leaned back and looked under the table. "Is that a new lunch box?" he said.

"No," said Tommy Pepper. He dropped the chain over his head and tucked it beneath his shirt. It felt warm. It felt like it had been made for him.

"Is that an Ace Robotroid Adventure lunch box?" said James Sullivan—and he wasn't saying it because he wanted to know.

Patrick Belknap leaned back too. "It sure looks like one," he said.

Tommy Pepper closed his eyes again. Doomed.

He reached down and felt for the lunch box. The chain slid warmly across his chest. If only he could be somewhere else—like a galaxy or two away. Or at least someplace where grandmothers didn't give their twelve-year-old grandsons Ace Robotroid Adventure lunch boxes. He ran his hand over the front of the lunch box and felt the cheap metal buckle under his fingers. His grandmother had waited in line and paid a lot of money for something that buckled the first time you touched it?

An authentic Tom Brady–signed football did not buckle the first time you touched it.

"So that's what you were hiding," said Alice Winslow.

James Sullivan was snorting chocolate milk out of his nose. "I'd hide it"—*snort*—"too," he said. *Snort.* "Let's see."

Tommy grabbed the lunch box. He felt his doom weigh heavily upon him. But what else could he do? He pulled the lunch box out from underneath the table and laid it in front of them. "My grandmother . . ." he began—then stopped.

It wasn't an Ace Robotroid Adventure lunch box.

The whole thing had flexed and bent. It was shaped sort of like an egg, but balanced perfectly so that it didn't roll at all as it rested on the table. Where the red cape of Ace Robotroid had been there was now a swath of bright sunset—actually, sunsets, because there were two suns going down over a strange sea. And where Ace Robotroid had been holding his flag, a startling blue moon was rising, and it looked like it was spinning quickly. Really. Spinning. And in the last light of the two suns, and the first light of the blue moon, streams of silky fog hovered a foot or two above the surface of the water.

"What is it?" said Alice Winslow.

Tommy Pepper reached out and slowly put his fingers on one of the suns. Hnaef, he knew. How did he know? But he knew. Hnaef, First Sun. Hengest, Second Sun.

"Does it open?"

"Of course it opens," said Tommy Pepper, and he pressed on the two suns. The thing split open on invisible hinges and inside was his hard-boiled egg, still wrapped in a napkin. "My lunch box," said Tommy.

He reached in, took out the egg, unwrapped it, and slowly ate it.

Alice Winslow, Patrick Belknap, and James Sullivan stared at the setting suns.

After lunch, Tommy's class went back to Mr. Burroughs's room. Usually they went right outside for recess, but Mr. Burroughs always had ice cream cake when it was someone's birthday—and he gave out the Dumb Birthday Present. Not as dumb as an Ace Robotroid Adventure lunch box, but almost as dumb. Tommy walked back, holding the lunch box in front of him with both hands. It seemed that Hnaef and Hengest were getting lower on the horizon, and the blue moon—Hreth! The moon was called Hreth!—was rising brighter and higher. The fog had disappeared and the water was pulling out with the changing tide and the whole thing felt—he couldn't quite believe this—wet. It felt wet, as if his hands were on the water. Or in the water. He kept looking to see if it was dripping, but it wasn't.

He put the lunch box in his locker—Hnaef really was touching the horizon now—and he went into Mr. Burroughs's classroom to cut his cake. It was already melting a little around the edges and dripping on Mr. Burroughs's desk, but Mr. Burroughs still made everyone sing "Happy Birthday to You"—Patrick Belknap played his accordion—and everyone clapped and then Mr. Burroughs handed Tommy the cake knife. It was, as usual, a beautiful ice cream cake, mostly because Mr. Burroughs made it himself, and baking, he said, was the highest of all arts, because it was the only one that you could enjoy with the eye and with the stomach.

Every sixth-grader who had eaten one of Mr. Burroughs's cakes agreed.

It was all white frosting and yellow cake and ice cream sheets, and on top were bright balloons of every color with strings made of icing that led to pictures—also made of icing—of every single person in the class. There was Patrick Belknap trying to hold his accordion up and play it at the same time. James Sullivan spinning his authentic Tom

Brady-signed football. Alice Winslow holding a bridle for her horse—the horse wasn't on the cake. Jeremy Hereford eating a peanut butter sandwich to put on weight.

"Go ahead and cut it," said James Sullivan, and Tommy Pepper lowered the cake knife.

A few of them started to laugh when Tommy began cutting. Then the laughs stopped. Things got really quiet when Tommy held up Alice Winslow's piece.

"Oh my goodness," she said.

"Are you all right?" said Tommy.

"How did you do that?" said Mr. Burroughs.

"Do what?"

"That," said James Sullivan, pointing at the piece of cake.

Tommy put the piece of cake on a paper plate. He looked at it.

He had cut all around the picture of Alice on the cake. He had cut around her and her bridle. He had cut along the thin line of icing that led to her balloon. He had cut around the balloon. And then he had somehow lifted the whole thing out of the ice cream cake and put the piece onto her paper plate—perfectly.

"Do me," said Patrick Belknap.

"I don't know how I did that," said Tommy.

"Me," said Patrick Belknap.

So Tommy cut out the figure of Patrick Belknap with

his accordion and his balloon and his string. And then he lifted the whole thing out of the cake and put the piece onto his paper plate—perfectly. Again.

"That is amazing," said Mr. Burroughs.

Tommy felt that he should be amazed himself. But he wasn't. It seemed like the most ordinary thing in the whole world. He cut out James Sullivan with his spinning football, and then Harriet Pulsifer with her sheet music (she wanted to be a composer), and then George Bisbee with his microscope (he wanted to be the first person to see an atom), and then tiny Jeremy Hereford with his peanut butter sandwich, and then everyone else, and he put the pieces of ice cream cake onto paper plates—perfectly. And when he was all finished, Mr. Burroughs asked if he could cut out a piece where he wasn't tracing around the shapes, and Tommy reached over to a part of the cake that hadn't been touched yet and began to carve out a long funnel that curved and curved around itself and then flared out at the end, except that the top of the flare bulged and reached over the opening.

When Mr. Burroughs asked what it was, Tommy Pepper looked at him, surprised that he didn't know, since it was so obvious: It was a hanorah, of course—which is what Tommy told him.

"A hanorah?" said Mr. Burroughs.

Tommy nodded. He couldn't believe that Mr. Burroughs wouldn't know what a hanorah was—or that he would admit that he didn't know what a hanorah was.

Mr. Burroughs went over to the dictionary to look it up while Tommy lifted the hanorah out of the ice cream cake and put it on Mr. Burroughs's plate.

"Oh my goodness," said Alice Winslow.

"H-A-N . . ." called Mr. Burroughs from the dictionary.

"O-R-A-H," said Tommy.

"It's not here," said Mr. Burroughs.

Tommy walked over, licking his fingers. "It's got to be there," he said.

Mr. Burroughs shook his head.

"You play it after a victory in battle, and also after Second Sunrise on the first day of the new year," said Tommy.

"There's only one sunrise a day, Tommy," said Mr. Burroughs.

Tommy nodded. "I know," he said. But then, suddenly, he didn't know. Was there only one sunrise a day?

Patrick Belknap asked if they could eat the part of the cake that hadn't been served yet, and Mr. Burroughs—who was still at the dictionary—said they could if Tommy wanted to cut it up, which Tommy did. He decided that he should cut up the rest in straight lines, which wasn't as easy as he thought it would be. By the time he was done, he was sweating a little bit—probably because it was such a warm day. He decided he had better give the cake knife back to Mr. Burroughs, who had pulled out another dictionary from his desk drawer and was looking through the *H*s.

He never did find *hanorah*.

But he did give Tommy Pepper his Dumb Birthday Present. It was a saltshaker. No one laughed. They were too filled with amazement to laugh.

That afternoon, Tommy walked home with his lunch box—or whatever it was now—in one hand, and his sister's hand in his other. Patty was in first grade, and she knew the way home and didn't need to hold on to her brother's hand. She even knew how to take the bus home, except taking the bus meant she had to ride with Cheryl Lynn Lumpkin and her mouth. But there were days when they wanted to walk home together because Patty was a little bit scared—and not because of Cheryl Lynn Lumpkin. Tommy knew this. He held on to her hand whenever she wanted.

He never told her how glad he was to do it.

They decided to go home the long way today, and so kept on Water Street and passed by the pavilion for Plymouth Rock and crossed the parking spaces and took the steps down to the harbor beach, where the water of Plymouth Harbor was rustling up the tiny stones and releasing them, and rustling them up and releasing them. Tommy looked past the boats and the long spit that marked the end of the harbor, and then out toward the bent horizon where the faraway buoys were tolling. And Tommy Pepper realized that he missed something. He missed it terribly.

Patty let go of his hand and started to poke around the dark and shining mussel beds.

He missed the second sun.

He missed Hengest.

And the sky was entirely the wrong color. The blue was so dark for this time of day.

He took his notebook from his backpack and pulled out a sheet of paper. Then he searched around in the backpack for something to draw with. He could find only a stubby pencil, but it would have to do. Quickly he sketched in the horizon—with Hengest shining too—and then he drew in the spit of land, the harbor, the boats. He drew in the ripples of the water. He drew in the tangy scent of the dark mussel beds. And he drew in the sound of the stones being pulled back and forth and the tolling of the buoys. And he drew in Patty, poking among the shells, and the tiny crabs underneath that she couldn't see, and the way they were scuttling back and forth, and the tidewater that had seeped below the sand and was dragging it out in etched canals. He drew in the iodine smell of the seaweed, and how the seaweed waved back and forth under the water when the tide came in. He drew in . . .

Tommy stopped. He blinked. He made his hand move away from the paper. He tried to open his fingers, tried again, and finally got them to drop the pencil.

He looked at what he had drawn. He listened to it. He smelled it. He felt it.

Then, quickly, he crumpled it all up. The sound of the grinding stones grew less, less, less, then nothing. He stuffed the crumpled paper into his backpack. He left the stubby pencil lying on the sand.

"Patty," he called, and held his hand out to her.

She looked at him.

His hand was trembling a little.

Tommy and his sister walked home quickly—until Patty started to run to keep up, and Tommy slowed down. Every time they stopped at a corner, the iodine smell of the seaweed came up to him, and he couldn't tell if the smell was on the wind coming inland, or if it was coming from his backpack. He decided not to take a chance, and when they passed a trash can, he took out the crumpled paper and threw it away. He thought he heard the sound of pebbles pushed by water as it fell. And was the tolling only from the buoys out in the harbor?

They walked past the neat boutiques and shops with flower boxes filled with late petunias, past all the restaurants for tourists and the parking lots for tourists and the trim information booths for tourists, and past the long green lawns of those who could afford to live in big white houses by the sea—past all the smaller houses with not such long green lawns, and then smaller houses with very little lawns, and then smaller houses with hardly any lawns at all and hemmed in by scraggly hedges.

And when those houses gave out, the road sort of coughed, stuttered, and then died into a gravel path that went up sharply into the sand, passing the sign advertising PILGRIMWAY CONDOMINIUMS COMING SOON! UPSCALE SHORE LIVING!

Beyond that sign, Tommy's old and lonely house tilted against a dune. It had no green lawn at all. Only scrub and sand all along the railroad-tie steps up to the house that had once been white, but the paint had blown away long ago. It had a center fireplace, and only a few bricks were missing from the chimney on top—which was also tilted.

The door squeaked when Tommy and Patty opened it, the floor of the front hall squeaked when they stepped on it, and the stairs squeaked when they dropped their backpacks onto them. Tommy thought that the house had been leaning against the dune so long, it was tired and ready to give out—something like his father these last few months.

Tommy had never once had a friend over to his wind-blown, leaning house. Patty hadn't either. Probably, Tommy figured, they never would.

Tommy went on back to the kitchen. This floor didn't squeak as much because it was covered with a layer of blue floral linoleum, but he could see through the holes in the blue linoleum to the red floral linoleum beneath it, and he could see through the worn patches in the red floral linoleum to the broad wood beneath. Someday, his mother and father had said, someday they'd take up the horrible linoleum. Someday they'd level the planks and sand them smooth as soap. It was a project his mother and father had wanted to do together.

Someday.

His father was there, making a birthday cake. A chocolate frosted chocolate birthday cake, which Tommy loved so much, it didn't matter that it was leaning too. "How was your day?" his father asked.

"Good."

"What did you do?"

Tommy went over to the cake and ran his finger along the chocolate icing that dripped onto the plate.

"Dug up dinosaur bones."

"What did you do with them?"

"Sold them to the Museum of Science in Boston for a small fortune."

"And your share of that is . . . ?"

"Five hundred thousand dollars."

"Not bad for one day's work."

"It only took a couple of hours," Tommy said.

"Not bad for a couple of hours."

"It'll do." Tommy walked over to the largest worn patch of blue floral linoleum over the worn patch of red floral linoleum. He crouched down and picked at it. "Do you ever wonder what the floor would look like if we pulled all of this up?"

His father licked the chocolate icing from his fingers.

"Do you?"

His father shook his head.

Tommy looked down at the patches. "I do," he said.

His father licked his fingers again, then looked out the window to the sea. "Your mother used to wonder," he said quietly. Then he went back to icing the leaning birthday cake.

"Should we try it?"

His father shrugged. He frosted the birthday cake.

It was always like that. One mention of Tommy's mother and there was nothing left to say.

Tommy went upstairs. He lived in the loft that spanned the whole house and which had been his parents' studio before he was born, his mother painting portraits at one end and his father painting seascapes at the other. Tommy wasn't sure how they both fit, since even though a loft sounds like a whole lot of room, Tommy could only stand up in the very middle of it—otherwise the ceiling came down to knee height over the floor. There was, however, a window at the south end that looked out over Plymouth, and a window at the north end that looked up the coast as it bent outward. So with the windows open, it was always cool in summer. And with the chimney squatting smack-dab in the center of the loft, it was always warm in winter—until the fire went down. After that, Tommy could see his breath shimmer in the freezing air.

And always, always, always there was the sound of the waves, the restless back-and-forth of the ocean, filling the harbor and emptying it, filling the harbor and emptying it.

That night, Tommy and Patty and their father cooked out on the dune. They heated up the clam chowder from the day before and dripped maple syrup on cornbread and boiled new carrots from their garden and poured out the first of the cider. Then Tommy's father and sister ran back into the house and they brought out the leaning chocolate frosted chocolate birthday cake, stopping every few steps to pick up the one candle still lit and to light those blown out by the sea breeze. It was getting colder and darker, and already the first star was showing over the water—but Tommy didn't care. It was his twelfth birthday. He had been alive for four thousand three hundred and eighty-three days. He had been alive with his mother for four thousand one hundred and twenty-six of them. He had been alive without his mother for two hundred and fifty-seven of them.

In the dark, the chain around his neck glowed softly beneath his shirt.

His father and Patty got the leaning chocolate frosted chocolate birthday cake to the firepit with some of the candles still lit. Patty had brought plates and forks and the Birthday Cake Knife, which Tommy took.

"Wait a minute!" said his father. "We have to sing before you cut it."

So he did. "Happy birthday to you! Happy birthday to you!" he sang, and Patty swayed side to side with the rhythm, smiling, and the sea breeze stroked the blue-gold-red embers bright.

And with that wind in his face, and looking at the sea, and feeling the light fall on him from the first star, and with those he loved beside him, and his mother gone, gone, Tommy felt the chain warm, and he began to sing too. He sang of parting and of grief. He sang of friends and loved ones who must leave him. He sang of the loneliness of one star without another. He sang in a high keen, as high-pitched as wind, and he felt the melody twine with the strange starlight, and heard the sound of Hreth rising out of the ocean, and he sang of that too.

And when he finished, he looked at his father and at Patty, who stared at him in amazement and wonder. And he saw in his sister's eyes that she was a little afraid.

"What?" he said.

THREE

The Wrath of the Lord Mondus

T*hen the wrath of the Lord Mondus kindled against Young Waeglim, the last of the Faithful Valorim, who neither trembled nor faltered in the Council Room of the Ethelim. Great was the anger of the Lord Mondus and great the torment he promised. Even the hearts of the O'Mondim—if hearts they had—moved with pity.*

And when Young Waeglim would not reveal where he had sent the Art of the Valorim, the Lord Mondus imprisoned him deep beneath the Reced, where the Twin Suns never shone, where the soft moonlight of spinning Hreth never glimmered. Young Waeglim did not tremble at his lonely doom, but as he was carried down from the Tower, lower and lower into the depths of the Reced, his eyes searched out each window, as if he might take within himself its light. And when he came at last to the final pane, then it was that Young

Waeglim burst upon the O'Mondim with the might of twelve, and more than a few of the Faceless would never again feel the covering of the cool sea. But Young Waeglim was finally dragged below into the darkness, down to levels even the Valorim had never seen, but which the Lord Mondus had discovered through his Art. Down so that the glow of torches grew feeble. Down so that even the O'Mondim trembled at the weight of rock above them.

Down they thrust Young Waeglim into a cell with no light, and they knotted the door with ykrat, which none can unravel but the O'Mondim.

Young Waeglim closed his eyes, that the darkness without would not become darkness within.

But in the Council Room of the Ethelim, the Lord Mondus sat upon the First of the Twelve Seats of the Ethelim. And he gathered a new Council, a Council of faithless Valorim. So on the Seats came to sit Saphim, second of the Twelve, whose cruelty was lesser only than that of the Lord Mondus. And Taeglim and Yolim, brothers of the heart who betrayed the Valorim at Brogum Sorg Cynna, but to no avail. And Ouslim the Liar, Calorim the Greedy, and Verlim, known as the Destroyer. And there were Belim and Belalim the Scarred, Remlin, and Naelim, the bane of Ecglaeth. And the last of the Twelve, Fralim, who was blind.

These were the Councilors who took the Twelve

Seats. Word of their rise spread across the world, and the Ethelim lamented that they had lived to see such days.

Yet the triumph of the Lord Mondus brought no joy to a bitter heart. He brooded upon the Art of the Valorim and pondered how he might bring Young Waeglim to reveal its hiding place. For of all of their treasures, it was the Art of the Valorim that was most precious—and most powerful—and the heart of the Lord Mondus longed to hold it for his own.

Then did Taeglim and Yolim come before the Lord Mondus. The one was tall and fair, and his speech was smooth as warmed melus. The other was hob-backed, and his eyes the black of old ice, and as cold.

The Lord Mondus unveiled the desire of his heart to them. "I would have the Art of the Valorim in my hand," he said.

"We need only force Young Waeglim to reveal where he has sent it," said Yolim.

"He would die first."

"Then," said Yolim, "let him die."

But Taeglim reached over to the shoulder of his companion. "So should we be without the Valorim Art forever," he said. "There is another way to the heart of one who has seen so little of the world."

The Lord Mondus sat forward in the Seat of the First.

"Send us down to the deep cell of Young Wae-glim," said Taeglim. "Let us be clothed as rebels to your reign, with no orluo, no armor, no sign of nobility as we bear. Let us be brought there by the O'Mondim and left in the darkness with Young Waeglim."

"What then?" said the Lord Mondus.

"His loneliness and despair will writhe around him like taloned vitrio," said Taeglim, "and to whom will he turn but us? So shall he open his heart, and so shall we find the place where the Art of the Valorim lies."

The Lord Mondus was well pleased.

So Taeglim and Yolim were taken to the cell, the ykrat unknotted, and the door opened. The darkness was so great that even the feeble torchlight blinded Young Waeglim within, but he heard the sliding steps of the O'Mondim, and the cries of the two, and their mock despair. And he heard the cell door clang shut and the ykrat knotted again.

"Friends," said Young Waeglim, "tell me who you are."

And Taeglim told how they had rebelled against the Lord Mondus, and how the battle had been terrible, and how they had been routed, captured, and condemned.

"The anger of the Lord Mondus," said Yolim, "is swift and sure."

Then they sat together in the darkness, as silent as the air around them.

But Young Waeglim sat a little apart.

And far away, the boy Ealgar, who would be called the Bold, began to dream.

FOUR

Yellow Flags

In the morning, Tommy heard the kettle whistling—
same as always. He threw on a sweatshirt, wrapped a
wool blanket around himself, and came down from his
loft just as Patty came out of her bedroom, yawning, and
he tousled her hair and she shook her head as though she
was angry but she wasn't. They took the two big mugs of
hot chocolate steaming in the kitchen and went outside
onto the dune, where their father had already kindled the
embers left from last night. He sat beside them and sipped
at a cup of tea.

Then they watched. It was a new show every time.
First they could see the waves close in and whiter tops
curling farther out. Then somehow the dark turned to
purple, then to a lighter and lighter purple, and the stars
thought about running in to hide. But you could never

look at a star and watch it disappear. Stars waited until you weren't looking, then skedaddled.

And then there was the horizon stretching like a smile and breathing out pinks and yellows and oranges, and everything was becoming brighter and brighter until suddenly, suddenly—Patty pointed—there it was, the sun's crest, tipping each wave's frothy top with amethyst.

Tommy and Patty and their father clinked their mugs together. Patty pushed her hair back and smiled. "Good morning," Tommy's father said. "Good morning," Tommy said—the first words they'd spoken.

The three of them had done the dawn together for two hundred and fifty-seven mornings. They hadn't missed one.

And on some days—like today—Tommy wished Patty would say "Good morning" like it was the most natural thing in the whole world.

But she didn't.

And on some days—like today—as he watched his father peering out at the ocean's colors, his eyes bright, his hands almost twitching, Tommy wished he would set up his easel again.

But he didn't.

When a cold and wet sea fog blurred the sun, they went in for breakfast and Tommy and Patty got ready for school while their father packed lunches. ("Tommy, where's your lunch box?" "I left it at school." "All I've got is a brown paper bag." "Dad, that's okay.") And since the fog was wading ashore, getting everything a whole lot colder and a whole lot wetter, they decided to take the bus, and Tommy and Patty hurried down to the end of the gravel path and waited a minute or two before the bus lumbered out of the wet. They climbed on and fell into the cracked vinyl of the seats and bumped toward town.

It was one of those days—one of the many days— when the heater wasn't working on the bus and Tommy could blow out and see his breath, which is what Patty did when they sat down.

It was also one of those days when Cheryl Lynn Lumpkin and her mouth were on the bus with them.

They could tell right away that she was there. She had a voice louder than three trempo together, thought Tommy—and that was saying something. One trempe could scare a vitrie from the sky. Three trempo could shatter an iceberg. And this morning, Cheryl Lynn Lumpkin was using her three-trempo voice to let kids who came onto the bus know they were wearing something she thought was stupid—at least, that's what Tommy figured started it all.

"Tommy!" Cheryl Lynn Lumpkin hollered.

He tried to ignore her, but you can't ignore a voice like three trempo—not when you're only three rows in front of it.

"Tommy, that jacket's looking pretty good for something you've been wearing since, like, third grade."

Laughter from all around the bus. Tommy sighed. How much longer was it until Christmas break? He stared out at the fog blurring the world.

"I bet it'll make it all the way through high school with only a few more of those patches."

"Go back to sleep, Cheryl Lynn," Tommy said.

"I'd like to, but Patty's hat is so bright. What color is that, Tommy? Siren orange?"

More laughter from all around the bus.

"I've never seen anything that color before. I don't think anyone's ever seen anything that color before."

Tommy Pepper put his arm over the top of the seat and brought Patty close in to him.

"Has she said anything yet?" Cheryl Lynn said. "Hey, Patty, how come you don't talk?"

Tommy leaned over Patty, and when he did, the green and silver chain warmed against his chest, even in the cold gloom of that early-morning bus.

Tommy felt Cheryl Lynn Lumpkin stand up behind him. He really did. He felt her stand as the bus stumbled toward Plymouth. Maybe because she was big. Even though she was in the sixth grade at William Bradford Elementary, Cheryl Lynn Lumpkin looked like she could graduate from middle school. Or even high school. And she could cuss like it too. And spit. And fight.

The chain grew even warmer, and Tommy felt Cheryl Lynn Lumpkin growling down the aisle of the bus toward them. He looked at Patty. He wished they had walked today.

"I heard that Tommy got a necklace for his birthday," Cheryl Lynn said.

Tommy felt his hand grip into a fist.

She was next to him, swaying with the bus. "Let's see your pretty necklace, Tommy."

"Crawl back into your hole, Cheryl Lynn."

"I said, 'Let's see your pretty necklace, Tommy.'" And she grabbed Tommy's hand and pulled it toward her.

Tommy grabbed his hand back. He was breathing hard.

"I'm not going to hurt you, Tommy. I just want to see your pretty necklace."

The chain grew warmer still.

Tommy imagined Cheryl Lynn Lumpkin sliding all the way down the aisle of the bus, legs and arms splayed out, her mouth a big squawking circle, her eyes round. Sliding on her butt. And everyone bursting into the loudest laugh the old bus had ever heard, and him looking at Patty and her leaning into him and saying, "Tommy, that was great."

That's what he imagined when Cheryl Lynn Lumpkin reached for his hand again.

What Tommy felt then was something he'd never felt

before. He felt his hand coming up—almost by itself—and his fingers spreading out.

"I don't see the pretty necklace, Tommy."

He felt his hand curve around Patty's frozen breath.

"Is that supposed to . . ."

But Cheryl Lynn Lumpkin never finished. She heard laughter from behind her—high, screaming laughter. She turned around. "What . . ." And then she heard the same laughter from the front of the bus. She turned around again. "Hey!" Someone mooed from the back of the bus and she turned around again. More screaming laughter.

Cheryl Lynn looked at Tommy, and then she looked behind her—where a thick, foggy back end of a cow was attached.

"Hey!" she said again. She waved her hand through it, but it re-formed and stayed attached. She waved her hand through it again. Still attached.

"What do you think you're doing?" she shrieked at Tommy. He thought that's what she shrieked, anyway. It was hard to hear on the bus.

Another moo, and Cheryl Lynn whipped around—it was amazing to see how easily the back end of the cow followed her—and she started down the aisle, and whether it was her foot or one of her hind hooves, Tommy couldn't tell, but she tripped, landed on her butt, squashed the back end of the cow into oblivion, and went sliding down the aisle of the bus, gathering all the slushy wet that the bus had accumulated during the morning run.

Everything happened just as Tommy had imagined it—except the last part. The very last part. The part he wanted most.

Then Cheryl Lynn started screaming—like four or five trempo. You could move whole icecaps with that sound, thought Tommy. So Mr. Glenn had to pull over to the side of the road and he had to go to the back of the bus and he had to try to calm Cheryl Lynn Lumpkin down and he had to pull her to her feet while she was still shrieking and then Jillian Donaldson said that Tommy Pepper had put a cow's behind on her and pushed her and the bus driver said he didn't see how it was likely that Tommy could put a cow's behind on her or push her all the way to the back of the bus and then Cheryl Lynn started shrieking like six trempo and Mr. Glenn told Tommy he'd better wait until everyone else got off the bus and then they'd see about things.

At the parking lot, Mr. Glenn opened the door by the first grade hallway and Tommy told Patty she should go on ahead—she'd be fine. Then Mr. Glenn drove around to the sixth grade door and slowly, kind of quietly, everyone got off the bus. Cheryl Lynn, who was rubbing not the smallest part of her, glared as she went by and used two or three words that mostly high school kids would use. No one else said anything to him, but through the windows, Tommy saw James Sullivan and Patrick Belknap running across the parking lot toward his bus—they must have heard—and they were smiling like Truth and Justice had triumphed. Which maybe they had.

"You'd better go on ahead and see Mr. Zwerger about all of this," said Mr. Glenn. "Not that it's anything. She must have stumbled all the way back there. But her being who she is . . ."

"Cheryl Lynn?"

"Rightly speaking, her father being who he is . . ."

"Just because her father's the lieutenant governor of the state doesn't give her the right to be a jerk."

"It's amazing how many people who control budgets that hire and fire bus drivers forget that. So you'd better go on into the principal's office. Let your teacher know what's what and I'll stop by to let Mr. Zwerger know too."

So Tommy, side by side with James Sullivan and Patrick Belknap, stopped by Mr. Burroughs's classroom and told him what was what, and Mr. Burroughs wrote out the pass and told him he was still looking for *hanorah* and was Tommy sure he had the spelling right? Then Tommy walked down to the principal's office, where Mrs. MacReady, the school secretary, told him he could wait in Mr. Zwerger's office and he'd be along in a few minutes and Tommy should not touch anything at all!

So Tommy sat down on the couch in Mr. Zwerger's office and looked around, not touching anything at all.

There was a painting on an easel.

Mr. Zwerger was working on a painting.

Tommy felt the chain warming against his chest. Again.

The black velvet shone under the office's fluorescent lights. A mountain scene with a goat and a fancy cottage stamped on in white lines. Numbers in the spaces between the lines. On the table beside the easel, a brush and fifty little plastic cups of paint, all numbered—like the spaces on the black velvet. Tommy went over to see.

Mr. Zwerger had finished about half of it, mostly the mountain and some of the fancy cottage.

It was, Tommy thought, well, rucca. Definitely rucca. Probably the most rucca thing he had ever seen.

He could fix it.

For a moment, Tommy thought that maybe he should not touch anything at all, like Mrs. MacReady said. But the painting was so rucca, he couldn't help it. He uncapped most of the plastic cups and picked up the brush. The cottage was ridiculous. There were all these little curlicues and decorated windows. A mountain cottage would not have little curlicues and decorated windows. He used the black paint to cover what Mr. Zwerger had done on the cottage, and then covered the black with a rusty brown, and then some gray, and blended it all together so the cottage looked like it had been standing against the mountain winds for a long time. Then he decided that the goat looked ridiculous too. He wasn't moving at all. Tommy dipped his brush into the gray again and took some of the white and then he redrew the goat until the goat was chewing and looking kind of thoughtful as goats do. Tommy adjusted the goat's beard to make him look a little, oh, jaunty.

Then he turned to the mountain, which looked ridiculous too. No one would build a cottage here if the mountain looked like that. He dipped the brush into the dark green and tinged it with some umber and he repainted the mountain so the peaks were low and round and the grass green and bowing under a brisk breeze.

Then he drew in the suns, and he got the light, light blue of the sky right. He stepped back, then painted in the short shadows of the cottage and the goat, and was stepping back again to see if the angles worked when Mr. Zwerger came into his office.

There were more than a few moments of absolute silence.

Tommy Pepper watched Mr. Zwerger's face.

He figured that Mr. Zwerger would be pretty happy. After all, the painting had been so rucca. So rucca it was almost fah. And now—if Tommy did say so himself—it was about as illil as any painting could get. Anyone could see that.

Except, apparently, Mr. Zwerger.

"What did you do?" he said.

"I finished it," said Tommy.

"I've been working on that painting for two years," said Mr. Zwerger.

"And now it's done," said Tommy.

"What happened to the mountain?"

"It needed—"

"And the cottage? Do you have any idea how long it took me to paint the curlicues on that cottage?"

"But they were—"

"Months!" said Mr. Zwerger.

Tommy decided that he would not point out how ridiculous the cottage had looked.

"And what is the goat doing?"

"He's chewing the grass."

Mr. Zwerger leaned in closer. "It looks like he's really chewing it."

Of course, Tommy thought.

Mr. Zwerger took off his glasses.

"He really is chewing it."

Tommy nodded.

"His mouth is moving."

Tommy nodded again.

Mr. Zwerger turned from the painting and looked at him. "How do you make his mouth move?"

Tommy was stunned. Wasn't it obvious? "You paint thrimble," he said.

"Thrimble?"

"Thrimble," Tommy said again. Everyone in the world knew this. Why didn't Mr. Zwerger?

Mr. Zwerger looked back at the painting. "How did you do this all so quickly?"

Tommy shrugged. He had no idea.

He wished that Mr. Zwerger could be glad the painting wasn't rucca anymore. But he wasn't sure that Mr. Zwerger was glad.

"Thrimble?" Mr. Zwerger said again.

Tommy nodded.

Mr. Zwerger walked over to his desk, still looking at the painting. He bumped into the corner and didn't notice the papers that fluttered down. Tommy picked them up and put them back on the desk while Mr. Zwerger sat down.

"I suppose you use some sort of computer chip," he said.

"For what?" Tommy said.

"For the thrimble thing."

Tommy decided to nod. It seemed easier.

Mr. Zwerger looked at Tommy, then at the painting, then back at Tommy. He coughed once. "I understand there was some trouble on the bus today."

Tommy nodded.

"Cheryl Lynn Lumpkin fell down the aisle of the bus?"

Tommy nodded again.

Mr. Zwerger looked at the painting. Then he turned back to Tommy.

"Cheryl Lynn Lumpkin fell down the aisle of the bus?"

More nodding.

"Did you push her?"

"I didn't . . ."

Mr. Zwerger turned back to the painting.

". . . push her."

Mr. Zwerger stood up and walked to the painting. "It really does look as if that goat is chewing something," he said.

"Grass," said Tommy.

"It must be grass," said Mr. Zwerger.

"I didn't push Cheryl Lynn," said Tommy.

"What?" Mr. Zwerger looked at Tommy again.

"I didn't push Cheryl Lynn down the aisle of the bus."

"Of course you didn't. I'm not accusing you, Tommy. I just want to know what happened." He looked back at the painting. "I can't believe how quickly you did this. Did anyone help you?"

Tommy shook his head.

"No one at all?"

"No," said Tommy.

Mr. Zwerger reached his hand out as if he was about

to touch the paint. "It's so . . ." Then he shook his head and turned back to Tommy. "Whatever happened on the bus, you've made a mess here. Why don't you take those cups of paint and the brush and wash them all out in the boys' bathroom. Be sure to get the caps clean, and don't let the paint dribble over the edges of the cups. Here, you'd better take the whole box."

Tommy did.

Mr. Zwerger turned back to the painting. "He really looks like he's chewing something," he said.

Tommy Pepper headed to the boys' bathroom. He wasn't sure he had done exactly the right thing with Mr. Zwerger's painting. But when he thought about it, he couldn't imagine doing anything else. He wondered how it might have looked if he had painted the mountain after First Sunset. If he had painted the mountain just after First Sunset, then it would really have been illil. He could have brought out the long shadows of the hills, and the lamplight flickering in the cottage window, and maybe the goat stamping his foot because of the cool breezes. And the mountain could have that kind of orange glow that mountains take on after First Sunset, when the light from Hengest is so slanted.

He opened the door to the boys' bathroom. No one else was there. He set the brush and the box of paints on one of the sinks and then looked up into the mirror. He saw the blank ceramic wall of the bathroom reflected behind him. Wide. White. Not really rucca, but certainly unfere.

Tommy Pepper smiled and picked up the brush.

Tommy brought the clean cups of paint and brush back to Mr. Zwerger. The principal was sitting in front of the painting. Tommy put the box down quietly on the table beside the easel and left, closing the door gently.

When he got to Mr. Burroughs's class, everyone looked up and started to laugh—except Cheryl Lynn Lumpkin.

"We were beginning to think Mr. Zwerger might have executed you," said Mr. Burroughs.

"That's what we were hoping," said Cheryl Lynn Lumpkin.

Tommy sat down at his desk.

"We're working on the circulatory system," said Mr. Burroughs. "So, Tommy, why don't you open up your book to page one hundred and fifty-two? Later, I'll catch you up on what we've already done."

Tommy nodded.

"Too bad he didn't execute you," whispered Cheryl Lynn Lumpkin.

"Too bad you were born," Tommy Pepper whispered, and opened his book to the circulatory system.

He sighed. He tried again to count how many days

until Christmas break. He flipped through to page one hundred and fifty-two, where there was a picture of a man wearing only his arteries and veins. Tommy stared at the picture. He felt his chain go warm. He picked up a pencil. He put it down. He was sure Mr. Burroughs would not be happy if he drew in *Science Today!*. But maybe, with a couple of strokes, he could show how the blood was rushing through all those arteries and veins—how it got pumped out bright red from the heart and then gushed to every part of the body, right to the fingertips, and then slowly got bluer and bluer until it ended up, kind of tired, back in the heart. It wouldn't take much. All he'd have to do—Tommy picked up the pencil—all he'd have to do is to start right—Tommy put the pencil down and reached into his desk for his pencil box and opened it and found the red pencil and the blue pencil—to start right where the blood came out from the heart—like this—and show where it was going—like this—and then how it got into the fingertips—like this—and . . .

Tommy felt his chain grow very warm. He drew quickly.

Then Tommy felt Mr. Burroughs standing next to him.

He looked up.

Mr. Burroughs was looking at the picture of the man wearing only his arteries and veins.

Mr. Burroughs's mouth was open. Very open.

Mr. Burroughs ran his hand through his hair.

He leaned down toward Tommy's book.

"Tommy," he said, "I can see the blood moving."

Of course, Tommy thought, and sat back, a little surprised, when everyone in the classroom, including Cheryl Lynn Lumpkin, crowded around his desk.

"Thrimble?" Tommy said weakly.

And that was when an office runner brought a note into the classroom and handed it to Mr. Burroughs—who looked at Tommy. "Mr. Zwerger wants to see you again," he said. "Something about the boys' bathroom?"

That afternoon, Tommy and Patty decided they would skip the bus and walk home again. They walked hand in hand, and Patty stayed very close. When they came to a corner and waited for the light, she leaned her head against him.

"You had a hard day, didn't you?" said Tommy.

Patty nodded.

They walked along Water Street again. Tommy looked out beyond the stretch of land at the other side of the harbor, out to the hazy horizon. The air was as calm as the ripples of the water, and he picked up a stone and chucked it past where the waves tipped over themselves. He could feel the stone flinging through the air, and the plunk of its splash was loud, and he could see—he really could—he could see it slowly spinning and heading down to the darker, colder water. He could see the shiny eyes of the little fish that watched its slow drop. He could see it settle among the sand and seaweed and brown muck and the beds of mussel shells with seaweed caught in their sharp edges. He could see it begin its long, slow wait against the push and pull of the tide.

Patty pulled at his hand and he looked down at her. She was watching him carefully.

"I'm all right," he said.

She took both of his hands in hers.

"Really," he said, "I am. But you know a good thing to do when we've both had a hard day?"

Patty smiled.

They went up the street to the coffee shop and Tommy ordered two hot chocolates, one with extra whipped cream, and they sat at a table by the window and they sipped and they watched shoppers walk by and tourists looking for Plymouth Rock and someone putting up posters for the Plymouth Fall Festival. And then Patty got a straw from the front counter and she put it in her hot chocolate and she looked at Tommy and she started to blow bubbles—big chocolate bubbles—and Tommy laughed.

He laughed as hard as he could.

Because Tommy Pepper couldn't show Patty how as soon as she had blown her first chocolate bubble, he heard his mother's voice saying, "Not in public, you doughnut brain!" and how he missed her like he would miss the planet.

When they got back home that afternoon, Tommy and Patty saw a new and much bigger PILGRIMWAY CONDO- MINIUMS! COMING VERY SOON! SALES OFFICE NOW OPEN AT LUMPKIN & ASSOCIATES REALTORS sign. Beyond it, bright yellow flags on bright yellow stakes divided the sand down by the shore. Another row of flags followed the scrub pines toward the front of their house and cut the dune into squares.

"What do you think they're for?" said Tommy.

Patty shook her head and they went up the railroad- tie steps.

Their father was not in the house. No easel set up in the living room.

Tommy made a honey and peanut butter sandwich and cut it in two while Patty poured the milk and fussed at the blue floral linoleum and then the red floral lino- leum. Then they went out to the first railroad tie to wait for their father and watch the waves come in.

But they didn't watch the waves. They watched the fluttering yellow flags.

Their father came home when the shadows started to get long and the sky turned the dark yellow that, Tommy thought, wouldn't be there if Hengest were still up. He was carrying a roasted chicken and a bag of sides and he bustled into the house and didn't look at the yellow flags and didn't talk about the yellow flags and didn't even seem to hear when Tommy asked about the yellow flags.

He carved at the chicken—not well. "We'd better eat this before it gets cold," he said.

"Dad," said Tommy.

"Let me finish, Tommy."

"What are the yellow flags for?"

"I'm almost done here."

He wasn't. He was making a real mess of it.

"Dad."

His father put the knife down and looked at Tommy and Patty. He looked at them a long time. "Your mother loved this place," he said finally.

They waited.

"She loved it more than anywhere else on earth."

Waited.

"It feels like we're about to lose her all over again."

That night, Tommy lay in his bed, twirling the green and silver chain around and around his finger. It was very warm.

He imagined all those yellow flags marking deep holes that bulldozers and dump trucks and huge loud machines with huge loud scoops would dig. Then he imagined the sides of the holes made into concrete walls, and then the steel frames coming out of them, and then the shingled roofs, and the vinyl siding, and the windows, and the flower boxes and mailboxes and garbage cans and people moving into the PilgrimWay Condominiums. He imagined his own house looking like a shed in someone's backyard. The dune, the beach, the waves, the smiling horizon out of sight.

Then Tommy held his chain, and imagined something else.

And in the morning, when they woke and went down the dune to do the dawn, all the yellow flags were gone.

FIVE

The Treachery of the Faithless Valorim

Many days, many days, Young Waeglim sat with no hope—for who was there to rescue the last of the faithful Valorim? Would the Ethelim dare?

He listened in the dark as his companions wept and roared, until one morning—if it was a morning—Yolim cursed the Lord Mondus and said, "What remains for us to do but die?"

But Young Waeglim replied, "Tyranny may be overthrown. The Ethelim . . ."

Yolim spat. "Waiting for weakness is a maeglia hope," he said.

"There is no strength left in the world," said Taeglim, "but the strength of those who rule the O'Mondim."

"If only we had the Art of the Valorim," whispered Yolim. "Then even the First Seat would shake and fall."

"The Art of the Valorim was not forged for such a task," said Young Waeglim.

"But it might be held to such a task," said Taeglim, "if the wielder had the will to do so."

"If we knew where it was," said Yolim.

And as the darkness grew thick and still again, Young Waeglim began to wonder. Had he done well to send the Art of the Valorim out of the world? Might he himself have wielded it, and in its strength, defeated the Lord Mondus?

Sitting on the First Seat in the Council Room of the Ethelim, the Lord Mondus twirled his rings. Already a force rose on the upper shore and Saphim sped northward with a great host. But unease labored in the Reced too. Spies told him of Calorim's secret messages sent on fleet wings to the west. Calorim he would keep close, the Lord Mondus thought. He held his halin tightly.

Young Waeglim and Taeglim and Yolim slept long in the darkness, and when they woke, the air was damp and chill, and they drew in hard breaths, for it seemed that they could not find enough air to keep them alive. Yolim fell to the ground with his hands to his throat, gasping.

And Taeglim spoke to Young Waeglim: "Do you

know where the Art of the Valorim is? We must leave this place. Nothing else will save him."

"It is gone from this world," said Young Waeglim.

"Gone how?" Taeglim said. He took Young Waeglim's arm. "How?"

Young Waeglim knelt down beside Yolim and reached his hands under his head. "I forged it into a Chain to send it far from the hand of the Lord Mondus."

"We must be out of here or we die," said Taeglim. "Is there no way to find it again?"

In the darkness, with Yolim seeming to perish by his side, Young Waeglim was moved with sorrow and compassion, and he said, "An O'Mondim who finds it may call back to this world, and so show where it lies."

"And is there no other way?" gasped Yolim.

"One other," said Young Waeglim. "One who receives it from a willing hand may bring it back. A willing hand, and a Song, and the beating of a great heart will make the Art of the Valorim stir strongly enough to bring the Chain and even its bearer across the stars."

Yolim laughed, and his laugh was blacker than the dark.

"But this may not be, for there are none of the O'Mondim outside our world," said Young Waeglim, "and no willing hand who knows of the Ethelim. The Art is gone utterly."

Yolim laughed again.

"You see," said Taeglim, "how even the longest hope revives the body?"

And Young Waeglim was troubled, for his heart told him something deep had gone amiss.

Three days later, Young Waeglim heard the sounds of O'Mondim coming down through the deep darkness toward them. The scraping of a foot against stone. A trunc against a thigh. Then the yellow light of torches upon the dampened air. The unknotting of the ykrat, the wrenching of the door, and Taeglim and Yolim were taken.

Young Waeglim listened for their sounds of despair. But only Yolim's laughter came.

So Taeglim and Yolim were brought to the Council Room of the Ethelim and the Lord Mondus asked if they had learned how the Art of the Valorim might be found. And they told him that the Chain of the Valorim might be found by an O'Mondim who would call to this world, and that it must be given by a willing hand— or perhaps by a hand deceived—and joined with a Song and the beating of a great heart.

The Lord Mondus was well pleased. And glad were the hearts of Taeglim and Yolim, for their reward would be great.

The Lord Mondus leaned forward in the First Seat. "Are there others who know how to find the Art of the Valorim?" he asked.

"*Only Young Waeglim,*" said Yolim.

Then did the O'Mondim guards take Taeglim and Yolim by the arms.

Then were sounds of despair heard as had never been heard before in the Reced.

So of the faithless ones who sat in the Twelve Seats of the Reced, Taeglim and Yolim were the first to vanish.

SIX

Tommy Pepper's Mother

This is how Tommy Pepper last saw his mother.

She was driving Tommy and Patty to William Bradford Elementary School.

She turned to the kindergarten side and Tommy waited while she walked Patty to the kindergarten door. Tommy saw her hug Patty, and Patty waved while their mother got back into the car. "Have a great day!" their mother called.

"I will," yelled Patty. She skipped inside.

Then they drove around to the other side of William Bradford Elementary and Tommy got out of the car.

"Don't forget," his mother said. "Piano lesson today. So take the bus home."

"Today?"

"It's Tuesday."

Tommy sighed. "I hate hate hate hate hate piano lessons."

"Everyone hates hates hates hates hates piano lessons when they're young. But when you're older, you'll thank me for making you take them now."

"No, I won't," said Tommy.

"Oh, Tommy, I love to hear you play," she said. "Especially the Bach. I want to cry when I hear you play the Bach."

"Me, too," said Tommy, "but not for the same reason."

"I want to cry because it's so beautiful," she said.

"I want to cry because of the crappy thing you're doing to me," Tommy said, and he slammed the car door, and even though he knew she was watching him, he didn't turn around, and he didn't wave, and he didn't yell back that he was going to have a great day. Not even when he heard the squeal of her wheels, which meant she was as angry as he was.

Good.

But that was the last time he saw his mother. And he never told his father, and he never told Patty, that it wasn't the ice on the road. He was the reason she was driving too fast, he was the reason she couldn't stop in time, he was the reason she . . .

He was the reason.

And he was the reason she began to disappear from the house, room by room. He was the reason her portrait of their family came down from the living room. He was the reason her portraits of her children came down from the front hall. He was the reason their father packed away her clothes, and her favorite books, and her music on the piano rack.

Tommy hadn't touched the piano since then.

Their father hadn't painted since then.

And Patty.

He was the reason.

Every time Tommy heard the squeal of tires, he wanted to run out into the road to stop her.

Every time he heard a car door slam, he began to cry.

Every time someone said how proud his mother would be of him, he knew she wouldn't be.

And he hated hated hated hated hated Johann Sebastian Bach.

Hated.

When Tommy and Patty got home from school, Mrs. Charlene Cabot Lumpkin, wife of Lieutenant Governor Lumpkin, real estate developer, president for eight years running of the Women's League of Plymouth County, and corresponding secretary (soon to be vice president) of the Mayflower Society, had driven to their house in her yellow Mazda and was standing in their living room—along with Officer Goodspeed of the Plymouth Police Department. Officer Goodspeed's face was looking pale, but on Mrs. Charlene Cabot Lumpkin's face there was more makeup than Tommy had ever seen on any one woman in his life. Parts of her were bright red. She smelled of sweet chemicals.

She glanced at Tommy and Patty, then turned back to their father.

Her long nails—red-light red—clacked as she moved her fingers.

"This house is an eyesore," Mrs. Lumpkin said. "It has been an eyesore for three hundred years."

"These are my children, Mrs. Lumpkin, Tommy and Pa—"

"How nice to meet you," said Mrs. Lumpkin. "Tell me, which of you helped your father pull up the yellow flags? Or did you do it all by yourselves?"

"I already told you what happened, Mrs. Lumpkin. Tommy and Patty, this is Officer—"

"Yes, you did," Mrs. Lumpkin said. "The flags all disappeared, just like that." She snapped her red-light fingers and her nails clacked loudly. "Magic," she said. "And tomorrow morning, just like that"—more snapping of fingers, more clacking of nails—"they'll all be back in the ground." She looked around at the three of them. "Let's hope they stay there," she said.

Patty took Tommy's hand and held it tightly.

"Perhaps then," said their father, "when the yellow flags go back into the ground, they won't be on our land. If you remember, Mrs. Lumpkin, we own down to the high-water mark, and—no, excuse me, let me finish—we own down to the high-water mark, and we will not be selling."

"Fair market value, Mr. Pepper. That's what Lumpkin Realtors offered."

"No, Lumpkin Realtors offered well below fair market value, and I refused—and I would have refused even if Lumpkin Realtors had offered fair market value, or double fair market value, or triple fair market value."

"Which is why we have filed for an easement so the town can assert ownership and finally make reasonable progress on our housing needs."

"And so Lumpkin Realtors can make a more-than-reasonable profit. Don't preach to me, Mrs. Lumpkin. I know the messenger. Tell your surveyors to keep your flags off our land."

Tommy's father put his hands in his back pockets. Tommy wondered if he did this to keep himself from strangling Mrs. Lumpkin.

"Fine," Mrs. Lumpkin said. "If you want your eyesore for a little while longer, fine. Between you and the beach will soon be the PilgrimWay Condominiums. We'll only lay out the easement. But you can't stop progress, Peter. It's for the good of the town."

"This isn't for the good of the town, Charlene. It's for the good of Lumpkin Realtors."

"It's the same thing," said Charlene Cabot Lumpkin, and she turned to leave.

"And, Charlene," said Mr. Pepper, "you still have not paid for your portrait."

Mrs. Lumpkin showed her very white teeth. "Your wife's work was shoddy, Peter, and I do not pay for shoddy work. That portrait doesn't look a bit like me."

Mr. Pepper shook his head. "No," he said, "I don't think that's it. I think it looks too much like you. But you didn't want a portrait, Charlene. You wanted a tribute."

"Didn't you know, Peter?" Mrs. Lumpkin showed her very white teeth again. "That's the same thing too." She left. The only part of her that remained was the sweet chemical smell.

Patty went to open the front windows.

Officer Goodspeed took off his hat and scratched his head. "She gives me a headache," he said.

"Tommy," said his father, "did you move the flags?"

"Not a single one," said Tommy.

"Patty?"

She was opening a second window. She shook her head.

"It wasn't me, either," said Officer Goodspeed.

Their father snorted a laugh. "I guess this means that there's someone else on our side," he said. "I wish I knew who."

"Can they really take our land?" said Tommy.

Their father walked across the living room and helped Patty open the last window. He looked out at the blue sea: the waves, the gulls, the distant mountain range of clouds. "I think we all need a snack," he said.

"A snack would be just right," said Officer Goodspeed.

The surveyors were on the beach the next morning. Tommy and Patty walked past them on the way to the bus stop. They tried not to look at them.

On the bus, Cheryl Lynn Lumpkin asked Tommy, as loudly as she could, "When are you getting out of your shack, Tommy? Or did it fall down last night? I'd ask your sister, but she's not—"

Tommy stood up and held out his hand toward her.

Cheryl Lynn's face whitened.

She didn't talk for the rest of the ride to William Bradford Elementary.

Tommy got off on the first grade side and watched Patty go in. "Have a great day!" he called. She waved. He wished she would yell back, "I will!" He wished she would, just once, just once, skip inside. But she didn't.

And she didn't look like she was going to have a great day, either.

Tommy walked around William Bradford Elementary to the sixth grade door, fingering the chain through his shirt. It had rained last night and the air was scrubbed clean and smelling enough of the ocean that he thought of seawater up his nose and the taste of brine and the feeling of sand all over him and the squish of seaweed underfoot and the roar of a high whitecap busting toward him.

Sitting on a scratchy blanket with Patty, his father. His mother.

His mother.

James Sullivan was standing by the door to the sixth grade hallway, tossing his authentic Tom Brady–signed football up and down.

"Hey, Pepper," he called.

Tommy stopped fingering the chain. He looked up.

"Go long!"

Tommy dropped his backpack and went long as James Sullivan lofted a spiral—a wobbly spiral, but still a spiral—across the parking lot toward the recycling bins. Tommy sprinted over the pavement, through a long and deep puddle, and barely caught the authentic Tom Brady–signed football on the tips of his fingers, so that James Sullivan, and Patrick Belknap, watching from the sixth grade window, and even Alice Winslow, who was also watching from the sixth grade window, started to clap. It was that spectacular a catch.

"He makes you look good, Sullivan," Patrick Belknap hollered.

"Kick off, Pepper," called James Sullivan, and Tommy kicked off, dropping the ball and punting it end over end until it bounced up in front of James Sullivan, who grabbed it and began to run toward Tommy as though he were headed for the end zone at Foxboro, which probably he thought he was.

Tommy ran through the long and deep puddle again—once your sneakers are wet, it doesn't much matter if they get wet again—and James Sullivan cut back so that Tommy had to cross the stupid puddle one more time, and when James Sullivan reached the end of the parking lot, he held up the authentic Tom Brady–signed football as if someone should hand him a trophy. "Touchdown!" he cried. "Touchdown with no time left. Sullivan fakes Pepper out of his wet socks and he wins the game! The fans go wild!"

Tommy went and picked up his backpack. "Real wild," he said. He clapped once.

Inside, the class bell rang.

"Kind of wild," James Sullivan said, and headed back.

But he stopped at the long and deep puddle.

"Hey," he said.

Tommy turned around.

"Look at this," said James.

Tommy went back. He looked down into the long and deep puddle.

In the still water, a sunny beach shimmered. Tommy could see the bright light heating everything up. Colored umbrellas propped in the sand. People sleeping beside radios and picnic baskets. A woman spreading suntan lotion on her legs. Two boys running down to the waves. And just coming up from the water was—Tommy looked closer—was a kid who looked like him. Wearing his Ace Robotroid bathing suit. Holding his Ace Robotroid sand pail and shovel. Quickly Tommy looked for the familiar striped umbrella. It was there, driven into the sand crookedly, and beneath it were Patty and his father and . . .

"That's wild," said James Sullivan. "It's like colors moving in there."

Tommy bent closer.

His mother?

His mother! And she saw him running, his pail full of seawater and starfish. She was getting up. He remembered this. She was going to come down to look at the starfish.

He remembered this!

She came out from under the shade of the umbrella.

And that was when the Southwest Side bus turned the corner of William Bradford Elementary and began to cross the parking lot, faster than usual because it was a little late.

James Sullivan looked at the bus. "Hey, Pepper," he said.

The bus driver honked.

"Pepper," said James Sullivan.

The bus driver honked again. Twice. Then again.

James Sullivan grabbed Tommy Pepper's arm.

"Just a second," Tommy said. His mother had almost reached him.

The bus honked again.

Tommy started to kneel down toward the puddle.

He didn't hear what James Sullivan heard: the engine shuddering and the brakes shrieking and the tires sliding against the asphalt. He didn't hear Alice Winslow and Patrick Belknap and even Mr. Burroughs yelling from the sixth grade windows. And he didn't see James Sullivan dropping his authentic Tom Brady–signed football.

But he felt James Sullivan jerk him up and away from the puddle.

The bus rolled past, sloshing and spilling the water across the parking lot, and squishing James Sullivan's authentic Tom Brady–signed football with its front right tire and throwing it under the rear left tire and ripping open almost all the seams, and missing Tommy Pepper's butt by not much.

When Tommy looked back, the puddle was all gone.

"Are you crazy?" hollered James. "Did you want to get run over?"

It was all gone.

"Didn't you see that bus?" yelled James Sullivan.

Everything was gone.

James Sullivan bent down to pick up the corpse of his Tom Brady–signed football, but Tommy walked over to the sixth grade door and went inside. He hung his jacket in his locker, put his books up, and went into Mr. Burroughs's classroom, where everyone turned to look at him.

He sat down at his desk.

"Tommy?" said Alice Winslow. "Oh my goodness. Tommy?"

He put his head down on his hands. He closed his eyes.

He didn't even see James Sullivan come inside.

It was the kind of day when you hope, you really, really, really hope the teacher puts on a long movie. It doesn't matter what the movie is. As long as it takes up most of the morning and most of the afternoon, it will do.

But it was the kind of day when Mr. Burroughs wanted to study the ancient Indo-European culture that gave rise to all modern languages, because it was over-your-head exciting. "*Polis,*" he said. "*Polis* is the word for 'city' in ancient Indo-European. Can you think of how the word *polis* has survived into our own language today?"

No one said anything.

Tommy stared at the posters of Fenway Park over the whiteboard.

"Has anyone ever been to Indiana and driven through its central city, Indian*a* . . ." He drew out the *a* for a long time.

No one said anything.

Tommy stared at the posters of Ted Williams and Tony Conigliaro and Carlton Fisk between the windows.

"Indiana*polis?* Or has anyone even flown to the city next to St. Paul? Minnea*polis?*"

Tommy stared at the the baseball in the glass case on Mr. Burroughs's desk—signed by Carl Yastrzemski.

"Tommy, where does Superman live?"

Tommy turned his head.

"Where does Superman live?" said Mr. Burroughs.

"The North Pole. But *pole* isn't the same word as *polis.*"

"No, it isn't," said Mr. Burroughs.

"Does *pole* come from *polis?*" said James Sullivan.

"No, it doesn't. At least, I think it doesn't," said Mr. Burroughs.

"So what does it matter where Superman lives?" said Alice Winslow.

"He lives in Metro*polis,*" said Mr. Burroughs.

"I thought it was the South Pole," said Patrick Belknap.

"No," said Mr. Burroughs.

"Wasn't it Krypton?" said Jeremy Hereford.

Mr. Burroughs ran his fingers through his hair.

Tommy bet he wished he were showing a long movie.

It was the kind of day when the cafeteria served Tuna Delight. With white cheese. And two asparagus spears.

And a brownie baked sometime during the ancient Indo-European period, in some polis very far away.

It was the kind of day when low clouds came in over Plymouth Harbor and shrouded the school with a mist that deepened until it began to pour, so instead of lunch recess, everyone stayed inside and read—except for James Sullivan, who stood by the windows and stared at the rain, holding the carcass of his authentic Tom Brady–signed football.

It was the kind of day when in Mrs. Low's Music Appreciation class, Mrs. Low played the Bach piece, the actual Johann Sebastian Bach piece, that Tommy used to practice. She played it much better than he did, and it was still awful. When Mrs. Low asked him why he had his hands over his ears, he told her that he had a headache—even though it was because the music was so rucca—and she asked Tommy if she should send him to the nurse, and he said no. Then she asked him if she should send him to Mr. Zwerger's office, and he said no. Then she asked him to take his hands away from his ears, and he did.

It was that kind of rucca day.

When Tommy picked Patty up at the first grade door, he could tell right away it had been that kind of rucca day for her, too. She dragged her backpack behind her and she didn't even try to keep her hair brushed from her face. She just let it fall across her eyes. She hardly smiled when she saw him.

"I know," he said, and squeezed her hand.

She squeezed back—a little.

"Do you want to go back home on the bus or along the beach?"

She looked up at him.

"The beach it is, then," he said.

Another squeeze.

So together they walked down along Water Street again, past Plymouth Rock and toward the shore. The rain had stopped and a cool breeze came off the water and blew at Patty's hair, sometimes so hard that she had to close her eyes against it. But Tommy barely felt it. He looked down at the beach and he could see it all: the sunlight, the striped umbrella, the Ace Robotroid pail, the shovel, his father, and right there—right there—his mother getting up. The sun was warm. Everything illil.

Patty tugged at his arm.

"Patty," he said, "do you remember the last time we were . . ."

And immediately, her eyes filled with tears. Immediately. Just like that.

What an idiot he was. What an idiot! He squeezed her hand again, and together they clambered onto the rocks leading to the seawall. They climbed all the way out, the low waves murmuring against the stones, and they tried skipping the clamshells that the seagulls had dropped at the seawall's end. Then back to the beach, and

Tommy stood while Patty bent at the edge of the water, picking up white stones, dropping them, picking up more, and every so often putting one in her pocket to keep.

Tommy took off his backpack, put it on the sand, and sat down on top of it. He started to finger the chain through his shirt. It warmed.

How bright and sunny it had been in the puddle. He could see himself in that stupid Ace Robotroid bathing suit. Coming up from the water. Plopping down in the hot sand beside the striped umbrella. Starting to build a sand sculpture. An octopus. Or a lobster. Or . . .

Tommy reached toward the damp sand.

He started to trace out a lobster.

Only it wasn't a lobster.

More like a squid.

But not a squid.

He knelt down on the sand to get the thing right.

Whatever it was, it had very long legs with knees that came too low. The feet were large and . . . webbed. Tommy sat back to look at it. Webbed was right. The chest was thin and long, but its arms were huge. Its hands hung down to its low knees, so in battle, it would be able to swing wildly. Tommy could imagine the whistling of a club, or a sword, or something worse.

Its head was round and large, but then again . . . Tommy rubbed away the sand. Not round. More jagged.

Sort of random. Like its long mouth. Other than the mouth—Tommy was very sure of this—it had no face.

He finished outlining . . . whatever it was, and started to pile the damp sand into the outline to make the body. He sculpted the strange long legs, the thin chest, the arms. He added a hooked weapon in its hand—a trunc. Of course a trunc. Then he built up the jagged head and left the face blank except for the terrible long mouth.

He stepped back and looked around until he found a scrap of wood. With that, he scalloped out the armor that covered the thing's body. When he got to the head, he added more sand from the shoulders up and shaped the tall, sharp helmet it wore.

Then Tommy knelt and added the halin that it would wear at its belt. He made the handle look like bone. The blade at the end of the halin had the same hook as the trunc.

Tommy stepped back again and looked. It seemed so . . .

An O'Mondim. It was an O'Mondim! How could he not have known this from the moment he started? An O'Mondim!

From over the water, the wind struck up and began to push the waves inland more fiercely than they had come in all day. Gray clouds began to scud above him. Sand blew against his face.

An O'Mondim.

Tommy stared at it. He couldn't take his eyes off it.

An O'Mondim.

He should destroy it. He should destroy it before the tide reached it.

He looked out toward Patty. Her jacket pockets were bulging and she was weighing two very large white stones in her hands, probably trying to decide which one she was going to try to fit in.

Tommy looked down at the O'Mondim again.

He fingered the chain.

Something was not right. There was more that he should do.

The tide began to come up. A wave almost reached the O'Mondim.

Tommy knelt down by the O'Mondim's head. He wiped the sand helmet away and reshaped the face quickly. Then he reached under his shirt and took off the warm chain and pressed it across the creature's forehead—deep, so that when he pulled back his hand, the chain's line was clear and sharp. He looked down at what he had done.

Another wave came, and this one reached the O'Mondim. It did not wash away the sand.

Tommy put the chain back on over his head. Hot against his skin.

Suddenly, the beach was very, very still. The traffic

from Water Street stopped, the seagulls lighted, the waves rolled dead.

And Tommy heard a moan.

It was low, quiet. He couldn't be sure he had heard it at all.

Then another moan.

This one he was sure of.

He had heard the O'Mondim.

Tommy stood.

A sudden wind came up. Tommy felt it hard against him, pushing him away.

With a jerk, Tommy Pepper kicked at the O'Mondim's right hand, obliterating it.

And the sound of everything started again—the traffic, the seagulls, the water. He listened. He couldn't hear anything like a moan.

He stepped back from the O'Mondim, and after a moment, he called to Patty. She came running over—sort of. She was pretty loaded down with white stones, including the two large ones that she couldn't decide between so both overflowed her jacket pockets. They moved up to the top of the beach and Tommy helped her choose the white stones she'd bring back—"Just three this time." Then they climbed the steps to Water Street, Tommy hurrying her. At the top, he looked back once more at the sand O'Mondim. The waves had reached its long legs, but when the water pulled away, it still didn't take any sand with it.

They hurried back through town and then along the gravel path toward home, which, when they got there, was surrounded by a new sea of yellow flags marking out foundations and roads and parking lots. There must have been hundreds of them. Thousands.

"You go on in, Patty," said Tommy.

She looked quietly at him.

"It's all right. Dad will want to see your new stones. I'll be up."

She pulled the stones out of her pockets, but she climbed the railroad-tie steps slowly.

Tommy went down to the shore, stepping around the yellow flags as if they were snakes with reared heads—and it wasn't easy, since there were so many. He looked far out to a horizon that was misty.

The sunlight, the striped umbrella, the sand pail. His father. His mother. Patty singing—he'd forgotten this!—Patty singing one of her songs that went on and on and on and that he would give anything, anything, anything to hear her sing again.

Anything.

So he began to sing of the grief of Githil, and though it was a song always sung for Hanathra, it came now achingly out of him, and the ache was so terrible that it closed his throat. But he sang against the misty gray of the air, and the misty gray of the water, and what was strange was that the melody of the song changed, and it became— how did this happen?—it became the Bach that Tommy hated. Githil's loss filled that new melody.

At the edge of the water, where the sea met the land, bearing the grief of Githil, Tommy Pepper sang until the end, when Githil climbed into his rau and floated away from the land and was seen no more in that world.

Then Tommy Pepper was silent.

His mother had almost, almost reached him today.

When his father came down from the house, they stood by the water together. His father sipped at his cup of tea. They listened to the tide. The waves troubled themselves.

"I miss her," said Tommy.

His father held him.

"I don't think even Githil knew what it felt like, missing her like this."

His father looked at him. "I suppose," he said. He held him tightly. Then, "We'd better head up," he said. "It's going to start raining soon, and it looks like the tide is coming in quickly." He looked at his watch. "Seems pretty early for that."

And it was a good thing they went up. They had hardly closed the door before the rain smacked against the house with a nor'easter fierceness too strong for early fall. Completely wrong. The wind bellied the waves into gray and white piles, and when they crashed onto the beach, the watery spume blew against the small Pepper house, which shuddered with each blast.

Tommy and Patty watched through the front windows. They had hardly ever seen the waves come up the beach this far, and they could feel the house shake when the water bellowed. Tommy figured that by now, the waves should have ripped the O'Mondim clear off the Water Street shoreline.

And he hoped that maybe the waves would take the yellow flags with them too.

SEVEN

The Woe of the Ethelim

Not many days after the hanorah had sounded in the Great Hall, Calorim the Greedy did fall from the walls of the Reced, and those who found him swore his hands were bound.

By Second Sunset of that same day, Belim and Belalim the Scarred were gone from the Reced—some said at the behest of the Lord Mondus. Others said that Verlim, known as the Destroyer, had commanded that they should march to the north. More whispered that Belim and Belalim the Scarred had fled to their ancestral homes in the west.

Whatever the cause, they reached neither north nor west.

The Lord Mondus commanded that the wuduo be hung for the death of Calorim, and Belim, and Belalim—as they had been hung at the deaths of Taeglim and Yolim—and that these Councilors be mourned, and that now the Twelve Seats would be Seven.

In the city below, the Ethelim watched the black wuduo blow in the wind, and the Lord Mondus heard their murmurs, and he reached out against them, whom once the Valorim had protected, and whom once the O'Mondim had gladly served.

At his word, the O'Mondim drew their trunco and did coil like vitrio around the City of the Ethelim. Those who remembered days of light felt the Twin Suns darken against them, for the O'Mondim smashed the glite of the houses in the city, they bore the mothers and fathers of the Ethelim from their homes, they left weak tears and vain rage. They tore down the bright columns of the Hall of the Valorim and laid waste to the beloit inside. Of the statues of the Valorim heroes they found, none were not ruined. Those of Elder Waeglim vanished as if he had never stood as iron against the faithless Valorim and the O'Mondim host at Brogum Sorg Cynna.

Then did Bruleath of the Ethelim, who had fought side by side with Elder Waeglim and had known his love, purpose to leave the city with Hileath, his daughter, and Ealgar, his son, for the foot of the Lord Mondus was heavy and Bruleath could not endure that the O'Mondim should come against his daughter and son.

Three days they watched the roaming O'Mondim,

and one night—long before the rising of Hnaef—the three cloaked themselves and gathered what was most precious to them and easy to carry. Behind their door, they waited and listened to the sliding feet of the O'Mondim, who searched for what was left to make fah. The breaking of glite was heard in the dark, and the stench of the O'Mondim thickened the night air, and still Bruleath and Hileath and Ealgar listened to the slything of the O'Mondim until it seemed that First Sunrise must soon begin.

But with rising Hnaef came the O'Mondim.

Bruleath did not hear them. None did know that O'Mondim could come on silent feet.

The O'Mondim burst the door locks. Then did Bruleath draw his orlu and strike down the first. But even as he swung the blade, even before the first O'Mondim was felled, there were trunco at the throats of Hileath and Ealgar, and Bruleath dropped his orlu to the floor and he was wrapped in long arms and taken.

In the empty house, it was Ealgar who picked up his father's orlu, and he and Hileath carried the fah fallen O'Mondim out into the street, and Ealgar turned toward the Reced and held the orlu with O'Mondim blood upon it up into the air. And then did he realize that his dreams were true dreams.

But the faceless O'Mondim dragged Bruleath through the city and up into the Reced. Through the

Outer Court they dragged him and into the Great Hall, and there they dropped him at the feet of Verlim, known as the Destroyer.

"Bruleath, hero of the Ethelim," spoke Verlim, "the Lord Mondus has heard how you once fought beside the Valorim and waged war against the O'Mondim."

Bruleath stood, waited.

"The Lord Mondus honors your deeds, if not their turn. Now he wishes nothing but peace to the Ethelim, and he would begin with you. He would withdraw the O'Mondim if you would turn the hearts of the Ethelim to his rule. It rests with you."

So did Bruleath, who fought side by side with the Valorim and who was sorely wounded at Brogum Sorg Cynna, hear the words of Verlim the Destroyer—and know them for slything lies.

"Bring me a sign of the obedience of the Ethelim. And know this: the Lord Mondus will not hold back his foot for long," said Verlim. Then did the O'Mondim gather around Bruleath and grip his arms and take him from the Great Hall.

The Lord Mondus stood in the uppermost chamber of the Tower of the Reced, where Young Waeglim had sent the Art of the Valorim out of the world. The song he sang was a dark song, and brooding, and empty, and it coiled away from the world like fast smoke. And the

Lord Mondus did not believe it would be answered, for how could it be answered when there was none to answer?

But he sang anyway, in dark hope.

And as Second Sunset fell upon the world, he suddenly raised his face to the cold air. And he heard the cry of an O'Mondim from a world where there could have been no O'Mondim.

Unless the Art of the Valorim had conceived it.

EIGHT

Storms

The storm kept on through supper and through dishwashing afterward. It kept on through Mr. Burroughs's circulatory system homework, too, and its shrieking was so loud, Tommy could hardly think about the difference between auricles and ventricles and whether white blood cells or red blood cells carried the oxygen and who cared how many miles of capillaries ran under everyone's skin? The storm kept on through making egg salad for tomorrow's lunches, and it screamed through *The Merry Adventures of Robin Hood*. Tommy's father had to almost holler to be heard—which didn't exactly make Robin Hood's merry adventures sound very merry.

Outside, the wind blasted the sand against the Peppers' house and pulled at the corners of the clapboards, tearing to get inside. The house creaked on its beams and the windowpanes battered against their frames until it seemed as if the glass must shatter. The rain came against them in such a flood—like the Falls at Hagor of Tillil—that Tommy wondered if it was rain or the waves themselves coming up against the house. He fingered the chain.

Then the lights blinked out.

"It's a good thing we built up the fire," said Tommy's father, and he went to the kitchen to find the candles and flashlight.

Tommy and Patty got off the couch and sat closer to the heat, side by side. Tommy felt the chain warm, and he looked into the fireplace and saw a hundred other fires he had watched there: fires on first days of snow, fires on Christmas Eves, fires with marshmallows, fires when their mom sold a portrait, fires when their dad got a show, a fire the night Patty was born, which he could barely remember, but there it was now, clear as anything.

A fire that terrible night, when they all three sat together without saying anything. It was raining that night—an icy rain. But not as hard as this.

Their father came back with the candles and set them around the room, and then he shone the flashlight onto *The Merry Adventures* and read until Little John knocked Robin off the log and into the water and jolly Robin had to wade to the bank with little fishes speeding hither and thither around him and had to admit to Will Stutely that he had gotten a dunking and a drubbing both.

So the storm blew on and on until their father said

they might as well sleep downstairs that night. Patty scrunched up at one end of the couch and Tommy spread out over the rest, and their father took two afghans out of the trunk in the front hall and he held them for a moment against his chest and then he laid them over Tommy and Patty and he blew out the candles.

Tommy watched the fire until he fell asleep.

And whenever he woke up that night, he saw his father tending the fireplace, keeping the room warm and bright until morning, and looking back at them, under the afghans.

When dawn finally showed itself, the yellow flags were gone again and all the beach was torn. The waves had reached up high and dragged sand away in long stretches, leaving behind shattered shells, broken crabs, tangles of rope and parts of old traps, and a layer of dark green seaweed that was already starting to rot. The red hurricane fences had been tossed aside and a row of old pines lay tumbled into each other and half covered with dark sand.

When Tommy and Patty boarded the bus to William Bradford Elementary School, they saw what the storm had done to the rest of the Plymouth coast. More pines uprooted and lying beside the road. New inlets dug into the beaches. Dunes leveled or moved wholly across the beach road. Houses with the shore eroded from beneath them, their porches hanging crazily in the air. And parts of the road mounded with blown sand. They felt the bus shudder and wrench when they had to plow through it.

Even Cheryl Lynn Lumpkin was quiet, watching the destruction.

Still, Tommy kept looking back, just to be sure that Cheryl Lynn Lumpkin wasn't intending to send a drubbing hither, so he hardly noticed the first policeman driving by with his siren going and his red and white lights turning.

He noticed the second one.

And the third, and the fourth, and everyone was at the windows when the fifth and sixth bolted past the bus.

"Looks like something's up," said Mr. Glenn.

When Mr. Glenn let them off at William Bradford Elementary, they walked across a parking lot covered with blown sand—sand that also covered the part of the school's roof that now lay across the TEACHERS ONLY! parking spots. The door to the first grade hallway hung splintered off its hinges and a whole lot of sand had blown in.

The door to the sixth grade hallway was completely gone.

When Tommy Pepper walked in, Mr. Zwerger was stalking the halls, looking about as grim as a principal can look—which is pretty grim. Tommy kept to the other side of the hallway until he got to his locker, where James Sullivan and Patrick Belknap were waiting.

"What's going on with Zwerger?" he said.

"Geez, Pepper," said James Sullivan. "Did you see that part of the school's roof is in the parking lot? How do you think he should look?"

Patrick Belknap leaned close. "And his house got robbed last night during the storm."

"How do you know?"

"Everybody knows. He didn't hear a thing because he was upstairs asleep. And whoever did it threw rotten seaweed all over the place. That's what woke him up—the smell."

James Sullivan clutched his new not–Tom Brady–signed football close to him.

"It's all right, Sullivan," said Patrick Belknap. "No one is going to steal your football."

"That's right. They're not." He stowed it under his arm.

When they got to their room, Mr. Burroughs was just as grim. His face was white and his mouth was drawn tight, and when Alice Winslow asked if she could get started on the day's word problems, he told her that she could wait along with everyone else.

Alice Winslow looked out the window.

Mr. Burroughs scattered a few papers around on his

desk, opened and closed a few drawers, went over to the board and picked up a marker, put it down. Then he went back to his desk.

"I'm sorry, Alice," he said. "I'm sorry to you all."

Tommy felt the whole class get very, very quiet.

"I'm completely out of sorts and none of you deserves that. The storm damage to the school is one thing. But . . . well, I guess even though it was meant to be a secret, you all know anyway: Mr. Zwerger had his home broken into last night and the whole first floor has been ruined. Drawers pulled out, cupboards all opened and everything thrown down—even the refrigerator emptied all over the kitchen floor. Every single dish broken. Every single book thrown into a heap, and since the front window was smashed to smithereens, all the books got rained on and seaweed dragged over them. And for nothing. It doesn't look like anything was actually stolen. Just some vandals who counted on the noise of the storm to hide what they were doing."

"Mr. Burroughs," said Patrick Belknap, "was his the only house?"

"Of course not, dummy," said James Sullivan. "Every single house in Plymouth got broken into. Didn't you smell the seaweed in your kitchen?"

Tommy saw Patrick Belknap glance back at his accordion case. He figured he wouldn't let it out of his sight for a while.

Mr. Burroughs shook his head. (Tommy knew that if it had been any other day, Mr. Burroughs would have done a whole lot more than shake his head, since James Sullivan had called Patrick Belknap a dummy, and Mr. Burroughs would have been all over him for that—if it had been any other day.) "Mr. Zwerger's house wasn't the only one. At least half a dozen houses on the coast were broken into and pretty much the same thing done to them. Everything opened and smashed. And this horrible rank seaweed everywhere. But maybe that's because of the storm."

The chain warmed against Tommy's chest.

Tommy shook his head. "Not because of the storm," he said.

Mr. Burroughs looked at him.

"Tommy," said Mr. Burroughs, "did something happen at your house last night?"

"No," he said.

Didn't they know about the fah smell of the O'Mondim? Tommy wondered. Didn't they know?

"Enough of this," said Mr. Burroughs. "Let's start the day again. With something cheerful."

"You don't mean . . ." said Alice Winslow.

"Patrick, why don't you go get your accordion?" said Mr. Burroughs.

Patrick Belknap rushed to get his accordion. Everyone groaned.

"Something you can tap your toe to," said Mr. Burroughs.

"Something you can throw up to," said James Sullivan.

So Patrick Belknap started playing and everyone groaned again, even though they were all sort of glad to hear him.

In the afternoon, Patty wanted to go home on the bus, but Tommy walked with her to the shore. They stayed up on Water Street and didn't go down onto the beach. They only looked—and only long enough for Tommy to see that the O'Mondim he had sculpted was gone.

The chain was cold on his chest.

"Patty," he said, "don't ever go down to the water unless I'm with you, okay?"

She looked at him.

"You've got enough white stones for now."

They walked home. Tommy watched the ocean the whole time.

He wondered if something might be watching back.

That weekend, and in the days that followed, a whole lot of people might have been glad to hear Patrick Belknap's cheerful accordion, because every night, every single night, terrible winds blew off the ocean and into Plymouth, bellowing so loudly that the noise was louder than doors thrown open, and louder than closets and pantries emptied, and louder than rooms ruined with rank and rotting seaweed. First, houses along the coast were attacked, and the police began to send out seven patrol cars each night. Then houses farther from the shore were ruined, and Officer Goodspeed began to look pretty drawn, and two policemen from Sandwich came up to help patrol. And then one night, the vandals broke into the Mayflower Society and Pilgrim Hall Museum up the street, and the bookstore and antique mall and coin shop between them. With the roaring of the winds, no one heard.

In the mornings now, everyone in Plymouth gathered around the news telecast to find out which houses had been targeted.

Officer Goodspeed looked like he wasn't sleeping. And two more policemen from Brewster came up to help patrol.

But everywhere, people were afraid.

And still the nightly winds tormented, and in the early morning, the smell of seaweed lay all over Plymouth.

But the days!

That fall was the most spectacular fall Tommy Pepper could remember—exactly the kind his mother had loved. Easy breezes in the morning, but cool enough at the dawn fires that Tommy and Patty had to wear the wool blankets. A bright sun that grew dark yellow at suppertime and threw long shadows across anything that lay flat. The beaches copper in the slanting light.

And the leaves!

Tommy and Patty should be sitting at the kitchen table, with new scrapbooks open and their *Field Guide to Trees and Shrubs of New England* at the ready, their mother softly handling the bright shapes—the red maples, the yellow sassafras, the scarlet oaks. Patty should be clipping off the corners of envelopes to mount the leaves into the scrapbooks—the mottled sycamores, the red and white pine needles, the golden birch. They should be turning each page carefully, carefully, so as not to crinkle the drying leaves—the rusty beeches, the browning ashes, the blushing apples. Their mother should be smiling.

It was that kind of fall.

Perfect, perfect, perfect for the Plymouth Fall Festival.

But hardly anyone in Plymouth noticed.

They were waiting for the shrieking winds at night. And what came with them.

A week after the storms, Tommy's father rented a chain saw and cut up the downed pines. Then, Saturday morning, they burned the sappy branches on the beach. And as the branches turned to embers, Mrs. Lumpkin's surveyors came to plant the yellow flags—again. Mrs. Lumpkin herself drove up in her yellow Mazda to watch. She never looked at Tommy Pepper's home, not once the whole time. If she had, she might have seen Tommy and Patty watching through the front windows.

On Sunday afternoon, the Peppers raked up the rotting seaweed below their house—rucca!—and the broken crabs and shells, and buried it all beneath the sand. They set up the red hurricane fences again, and the pieces of fencing that couldn't be fixed they burned on top of the pine ashes.

On Monday, Mr. Burroughs worked hard at pretending that everything in Plymouth was exactly as it was supposed to be—which might have been easier for him since he lived across the bridge in East Sandwich. But it was a lot harder for Tommy and everyone else to pretend, especially since on Sunday night, the steeple of First Congregational came down and its doors were thrown open and its pews covered with seaweed.

In Plymouth, everyone listened for the winds.

Even during the day, in William Bradford Elementary School, they all listened for the winds.

"Today, we're beginning our unit on the solar system," Mr. Burroughs announced. "Who can name the eight planets in order?"

James Sullivan raised his hand. "Do you think the storms have anything to do with all the houses getting broken into?"

"That is something the police are working on, I'm

sure, Mr. Sullivan. Let's let them do their job. Can anyone name the eight planets?"

Alice Winslow raised her hand. "The storms must have something to do with the break-ins, because they both began the same day. Whoever is breaking in probably uses the noise to cover their entry."

"Let's stay focused," said Mr. Burroughs. "Can anyone name any of the giant planets?"

"But how can they depend on storms coming every night?" said James Sullivan.

"Any of the inner planets?" said Mr. Burroughs.

"And what's with all the seaweed?" said Jeremy Hereford.

"Any planet at all?" said Mr. Burroughs.

Patrick Belknap drew his accordion close to him. "No one's going to touch this," he said.

"The planet we're on right now?" said Mr. Burroughs.

"Maybe we could use an accordion for bait," said James Sullivan.

Mr. Burroughs sat down.

That night, another storm. Terrible winds. High waves. And three more houses broken into south along the coast.

Then, on Tuesday, a house broken into in broad daylight—with no storm at all.

On Wednesday, four more in the afternoon—with no storm at all.

Three more patrol cars came, this time from Brookline.

But Plymouth began to be very afraid.

Though no one had made any announcement, the parents of William Bradford Elementary started driving their kids to school and back. Mr. Zwerger sent a letter home to let parents know that there would be bus service even during the current crisis, and he strongly recommended that if students were not driving with their parents, they should use the buses. Children should not under any circumstances be allowed to walk home alone, he wrote, even for short distances. And if they must walk, then he asked parents to form groups with chaperones.

And that was how someone finally broke into Tommy Pepper's house.

Because while Tommy's father drove to school to pick up Patty and Tommy, and while they stopped at one store for the Styrofoam balls that Tommy needed for his solar system project and stopped at another store for Patty's new backpack—made of some vinyl-y stuff colored the brightest pink that the human eye can endure—and while they stopped at the A&P for a roasted chicken, macaroni salad, tomatoes, mozzarella cheese, and a pineapple, someone entered their house.

When Tommy and Patty and their father got back

home, they didn't have to open the door—which had been torn off and broken in two—to smell the rotten seaweed that lay all over the floors. One look and Tommy's father pushed Tommy and Patty outside while he phoned into town. But Tommy saw everything in that one look: the thrown-down shelves, the overturned chairs, the emptied cabinets, the books opened and stained green, the piano pulled away from the wall, the walls with holes punched through to the framing.

Tommy sat with Patty on one of the pine stumps while the policemen came and went, came and went. Patty leaned against him, her eyes closed so she didn't see the lights on top of the police cars—all ten of them.

But you can't have that many police cars with their lights going crazy without someone seeing, and pretty soon James Sullivan with his not–Tom Brady–signed football and Patrick Belknap with his accordion strapped to his back were on the dune. Even Alice Winslow came up, and she sat on the sand and took Patty in her lap and tied her hair in braids.

Tommy could almost not bear to watch them. He remembered.

His chain was warm.

He knelt down and swept the sand with his palms until it was flat. With two fingers, he dug around the smoothed sand, dragging up the darker sand into a frame around it. He looked again at Alice Winslow and Patty and he began to draw inside the frame, using only his two thumbs. On one side he drew Patty, sitting calmly in Alice's lap, but a little younger than she was now, her head bent back a little, her smile. And beside her, on the other side, he drew Alice, leaning over Patty, working gently at her hair, intent.

James Sullivan stopped twirling his not–Tom Brady–signed football. "That's amazing," he said. "Pepper, how can you do that?"

Alice Winslow and Patty got up and came around to see the picture.

"That's you two," said Patrick Belknap.

"It's Patty," said Alice Winslow, shaking her head. "But not me."

And she looked at Tommy in perfect understanding.

It wasn't her.

When Tommy and Patty went up to the house, Officer Goodspeed had his hat off and his hand up to the back of his neck. He was shaking his head. "I don't think this could be Mrs. Lumpkin," he was saying.

"I'm not saying she did it herself," said Tommy's father. "She probably hired someone else to do it for her."

"She's the wife of the lieutenant governor."

"She's the ruthless wife of a ruthless lieutenant governor. Look—she's the only one in all of creation besides us who wants this house. Why else would anyone come inside? There's nothing that we have that anyone would want."

"Who knows why someone would vandalize a house?"

"This isn't just vandalism, Mike. Have any of the other houses been torn apart as completely as this one? Look at the studs."

"Mr. Zwerger's, maybe."

"Anyone else's?"

Officer Goodspeed rubbed the back of his neck again.

"I guess not," he said.

Officer Goodspeed drove down to Lumpkin and Associates Realtors, and when he came back up at suppertime, he told the Peppers how he had said to Mrs. Lumpkin that he didn't even imagine she had anything to do with the wrecked Pepper house, but would she mind answering a few questions anyway? Mrs. Lumpkin had told Officer Goodspeed that she certainly did mind answering a few questions anyway and was this something that Mr. Pepper had put him up to in order to tarnish her reputation because Mr. Pepper had sworn to do whatever it took to stop the PilgrimWay Condominiums and this was just what she might expect from someone like Mr. Pepper who didn't care a tinker's curse about the town's housing needs.

Officer Goodspeed told her there had been an unusual amount of damage in the Peppers' house and everyone knew—

That explains everything, said Mrs. Lumpkin, because Mr. Pepper was certainly capable of wrecking his own house if he thought it might discredit her but she wasn't going to stand for it.

"You know that's ridiculous, Mike," said Mr. Pepper. "I'm not going to ruin my own house."

"I know," Officer Goodspeed said. "But Mrs. Lumpkin claims you've taken up all the surveying flags twice now."

"That's ridiculous too."

"I know, I know." Officer Goodspeed looked out the front windows. "All the same, what did happen to those flags?"

Tommy's father shrugged. "No idea," he said.

"You kids have any idea?"

Patty shook her head. Tommy shook his head too.

Officer Goodspeed gave a big, weary sigh. "I don't suppose you could break a door in two, could you, Tommy?"

"I don't think so," Tommy said.

"Patty, you breaking down any doors lately?"

Patty shook her head again.

Officer Goodspeed laughed and reached out to muss up her hair. "I know," he said. "You cook that chicken yourself?"

They ate the roasted chicken, macaroni salad, tomatoes, and mozzarella cheese, and when Officer Goodspeed had toothpicked the last piece of the pineapple, he stood up, thanked them, promised he'd try to keep Mrs. Lumpkin off their backs—"How about off our property?" said Tommy—and told them he'd let them know if he found out anything.

Tommy doubted he'd find out anything.

Tommy and Patty slept that night in sleeping bags in their father's room—the only room that had enough windows to let out the stench of rotting seaweed. Sort of.

It was when Tommy took off his shirt and started to wriggle down into the sleeping bag that his father saw the chain.

"Where did you get that?"

Tommy reached up and held it. "It was in Grandma's lunch box."

His father leaned down over him. "It's glowing a little."

"Sometimes it does that."

His father took the chain between his fingers. "I told you Grandma always gave thoughtful presents." He rubbed the strands against each other. "Your mother"—he kept fingering it—"your mother would have liked this."

Tommy nodded.

His father let it go and Tommy scrunched down into the sleeping bag.

"Good night, Tommy. Good night, Patty." He kissed

them both, and then he lay down in the chair he'd dragged in front of the bedroom door. The night was warm—which was good since the front door was gone.

Tommy lay awake for a long time.

His mother.

His mother.

His mother would have liked the chain.

He listened to the night wind start to rise. Soon it would begin to shriek. He looked at Patty and saw her eyes open and staring out into the dark. He saw his father stiffen in the chair when the first strong gusts blew into the house.

Tommy fingered the chain, warm on his chest. Then he grasped it. Hard. He imagined the wind dying down into a breeze, and then the breeze dying down, dying down, down to stillness. He imagined the waves rolling gently, hardly breaking when they reached the shore.

Patty fell asleep.

Through the window, Tommy watched the stars curving their ways across the borderless dark sky and the moon coming up and he imagined the silver light of Hreth making everything soft and quiet, soft and quiet, soft and quiet.

His father fell asleep.

He felt a gust of wind, and he imagined holding it and laying it down along the sand until it, too, was asleep. He imagined gusts laying down their heads up on Burial Hill, and along Water Street, and beside First Congregational and Pilgrim Hall, falling asleep, soft and quiet.

And it was.

So he was almost asleep himself when he heard the cry rising from the Plymouth shore and calling toward the stars. A terrible, sad cry of someone whose sadness was beyond Githil's. Someone lonely and lost, calling, and afraid to call. Someone alone.

Tommy Pepper held the chain.

The O'Mondim was calling. Its heart was breaking.

In the morning, Tommy was up before his father and sister. He figured it was almost dawn. He went into the living room and opened all the windows that looked out to the sea. He looked around for an unbroken chair. None. He went into the kitchen and found one and he brought it back and sat down at the piano.

He looked outside at the ocean.

The chain was warm on his chest.

He turned back to the piano and held out his hands.

He played "Sleepers Wake!" The Bach piece.

He played the song beautifully.

He played as if the music were coming out of his fingers.

He played as if the music were coming out of his heart.

And when he finished, he turned and saw his father and Patty standing, watching him.

They were crying.

And he looked outside and felt the lonely eyes in the water.

At breakfast, he tried to tell his father.

"I think I know who's breaking into the houses," he said.

"Tommy, Mrs. Lumpkin wouldn't break into all the houses in Plymouth just to get our house for her condominiums. Even I know that."

"It's not Mrs. Lumpkin. It's the O'Mondim from the beach."

Patty put down her orange juice.

"The O'Mondim?" said their father.

Tommy nodded.

"What is an O'Mondim?"

"A race that the Valorim made come alive with their Art," said Tommy.

"A race that the Valorim made come alive with their art."

"Yes," said Tommy. "He's all alone. And he wants to go home."

"Probably he would," said his father. "And home is . . . where?"

"No one knows. Far beneath the sea, in a place only

the Elders of the Valorim knew when they first gave life to the O'Mondim. But they're all gone now. And only the O'Mondim know where it is."

"Maybe if we found it, it would be filled with dinosaur bones, and we could collect them and sell them all to the Museum of Science."

"I know it sounds crazy, but I think there really is an O'Mondim, and I think he's lonely and maybe afraid, and he's trying to find whatever it was that made him come to life, and maybe if he finds it—"

"Tommy, this is serious vandalism. This isn't something to make up stories about."

"I'm not making up stories."

"It sure sounds like one." His father sipped at his tea.

A long moment.

"Mom would have believed me," said Tommy.

Tommy's father stopped sipping. Finally: "Okay. What will he do if he finds whatever it is that made him come to life?"

"I don't know. Go home, maybe. So he's not alone."

Tommy's father took another sip of tea.

That night—a soft and quiet night—Tommy Pepper played "Sleepers Wake!" and then he went outside onto the dune and listened for the O'Mondim. But he did not hear him, and his father told him to come inside. It was getting late.

Later still, when he was sure his father was asleep, Tommy got out of bed. It was cold, and he held his arms around himself. He went outside onto the dune again, and since the bright moon was up, he could see all the waves. They rolled in smoothly and gently, one after another, singing their own song.

Then Tommy Pepper saw something happen.

Not far out into the water, it was as if a rock had risen. The low waves parted themselves around it.

Tommy watched.

And then he heard it: the Bach piece, coming from the water, low like the waves, gentle like the sea breeze, bright like the moon.

He listened.

The Bach piece.

Lonely. Like missing someone you loved.

Then it stopped. And instantly, the chain was hot. So hot, Tommy had to gather his shirt around it.

And a star streaked across the sky, staggered for a moment, then plummeted straight downward in white heat before it winked out.

When Tommy looked by the shore again, whatever had risen was gone and the waves rolled in again unhindered. The song was over.

But the chain was still hot, and Tommy knew that everything had changed.

NINE

A Journey Across the Dark

In the Tower of the Reced, the Lord Mondus rekindled the Forge of the Valorim, and for eight days and eight nights, as the Twin Suns rose and fell and burned their light into the fire of that Forge, the Lord Mondus fed the flames, and terrible they were to see, so that the Lord Mondus himself would have perished in them, but for his Art.

And on the eighth day, between the rising of Hnaef and the rising of Hengest, the Lord Mondus forged an arm ring from the orluo of Yolim and Taeglim, and Calorim the Greedy, and Belim and Belalim the Scarred, and dark it was and filled with the Silence. When the Lord Mondus beheld that ring's terrible shining, he was glad-hearted.

So at the last light of the day, the Lord Mondus called Verlim the Destroyer and Ouslim the Liar to him in the Tower of the Reced, and he said to them, "Mighty are you both. So you shall go find the Art of the Valorim and bring it back, that we may rule forever."

Verlim the Destroyer and Ouslim the Liar bowed low.

"The Art of the Valorim cannot be taken by strength of hand. It must be given. Remember this."

"It must be given," said Ouslim the Liar.

"And remember this too: When it has been given, destroy those who have learned even the least of its secrets."

Verlim the Destroyer and Ouslim the Liar bowed low again.

"Bring the Chain back and put it around my neck, so your deeds and bravery shall be known from generation to generation," said the Lord Mondus.

The Lord Mondus lifted the dark arm ring and clasped it around the arm of Verlim the Destroyer. In the torch-lit room, it gleamed brilliant as the jewels of Harneuf, and greater. "Let this be a sign to all who see it, that Verlim the Destroyer is my favored one, to whom I entrust this greatest task in all our world."

And Verlim the Destroyer bowed to the floor, smiling.

And Ouslim the Liar burned in his heart.

But the Lord Mondus turned to the Tower window,

where Second Sunset was swiftly growing darker and darker.

Then the Lord Mondus held up his hand into the red light of Second Sunset, and he sang out into the light, a song loud and long and terrible, and they felt the Silence rush into the room as a great wind. And the Lord Mondus commanded Verlim the Destroyer and Ouslim the Liar to stand close, and he sang again, and his song drew pale fire from the ring around the arm of Verlim the Destroyer, and the pale fire came around them both, and lifted them, slowly, slowly, until with sudden swiftness they flew from the warm air of their world into outer darkness, where the cry of a far-away O'Mondim still sounded in that cold space.

Blithe was the heart of the Lord Mondus.

So the faithless Valorim followed the cry of the far-away O'Mondim, hearts beating, Verlim the Destroyer holding fast to the arm ring of the Lord Mondus as they hurtled past familiar stars, and then stars they had never known or imagined.

But the time came that even as the O'Mondim's cry grew louder, Verlim the Destroyer and Ouslim the Liar found that the stars were passing less quickly, and the pale fire around them both was growing less, and they knew that the Art of the Lord Mondus was not the Art of the Valorim, but weaker, and their hearts feared that the pale fire would fall away and they would be cast down utterly. And so it seemed, for the stars stopped their rushing, and the fire sputtered as if it would go out, and they cursed the Lord Mondus for his weakness and for their downfall.

But not for honor had Verlim the Destroyer been given the arm ring forged by the Lord Mondus.

He felt the ring warm, and he reached to pull at it— but it would not yield for all his strength. Then it grew hot, and Verlim the Destroyer sought to tear it from his arm, but he could not, and the arm ring ignited, and with it, the pale fire around them, and so they were sent on again, speeding past galaxies after the echoes of the O'Mondim's cries, speeding with the death despair of Verlim the Destroyer singing in the ears of Ouslim the Liar, whose heart was blithe.

They flew and flew, their flight made swift with the burning life of Verlim the Destroyer. They flew and flew, until they came to a blue world on the edge of a small galaxy, and they followed the O'Mondim echoes down and down, the fire of the arm ring brighter and brighter and brighter against the darkness of that world's night, and with one last burst, they dropped straight down to a dark and cold shore, where the pale fire fell away from them, and where an O'Mondim waited in the water sightlessly.

So Ouslim the Liar came to the world of the Art of

the Valorim. But Verlim the Destroyer was only ashes that floated away in the waves.

And when it was known that Verlim the Destroyer would return no more to the Reced, the wuduo were hung for twenty-four days, and the hearts of those who still sat in the Seats quivered with fear of the Lord Mondus—but none would speak of it, for there was none to trust.

TEN

The Plymouth Fall Festival

A few days after the Peppers' house had been wrecked, Mrs. Charlene Cabot Lumpkin drove over in her yellow Mazda. Tommy saw her park on the dune grass, saw her check the alignment of the yellow flags as she came toward the house, saw her pause for a long moment to survey the view of the Atlantic that the inhabitants of PilgrimWay Condominiums would enjoy as soon as she could get their condos built. The sea fog was thick that afternoon, lying on the beach in big clumps, and Tommy watched Mrs. Lumpkin wonder if there was anything she could do to eliminate the nuisance of it for future PilgrimWay-ers. But finally she turned and climbed up the railroad-tie steps and knocked at the plywood across what was left of their front door.

Mrs. Lumpkin was very, very sorry to hear of their

trouble. It must have been awful to come home to such a disaster. She could see why they might have wanted to blame her, since in such a crisis, victims need someone to blame. She did not hold it against them. She was here to be of assistance. She could see that they hadn't even been able to sweep up all the glass yet. And clearly the damage to the hall wall was catastrophic. She doubted it could be repaired without tearing everything out and beginning again. And just look at the living room! She put her hand on the old center beam of the house. It felt a little shaky to her—and she had a Realtor's touch, you know.

Mrs. Lumpkin shook her head. She had seen less damaged houses condemned by the town and torn down.

Whoever could have done such a thing?

Mrs. Lumpkin pointed out, however, that lemonade can be made from lemons, that every cloud has a silver lining, that the brightest morning comes after the darkest night. She was prepared with the same offer, even though the house was clearly devastated. She had the papers out in her car. If Mr. Pepper . . .

Mrs. Lumpkin said that Mr. Pepper did not need to take that tone.

Mrs. Lumpkin said that her only purpose had been to come—in good faith—to lend a helping hand.

Mrs. Lumpkin said that no one had ever used such words in her presence before.

Mrs. Lumpkin said that she had never been treated so rudely.

Mrs. Lumpkin said that business was business but she would be glad to see the end of the Peppers in Plymouth and he could whistle for the payment on her portrait.

Mrs. Lumpkin opened her eyes very wide and half walked, half ran down the railroad-tie steps toward her yellow Mazda.

Tommy stepped onto the dune. His fingers spread out and his hand curved around the sea fog.

He felt Patty beside him. She was shaking her head.

Tommy uncurved his hand and let the fog go.

Mrs. Lumpkin drove away very quickly.

The Peppers went back to cleaning their house.

By the end of the week, the Peppers had replaced the smashed windows—no need to fit the new screens until next summer—and cleared out the broken furniture and brought in new beds and dressers for Tommy and Patty and repaired the kitchen table and three of the chairs, and they were only a little tippy. They'd hung a new front door and the wall in the hall had new sheetrock and was spackled and primed and ready for painting. Tommy asked for pale yellow—his mother's favorite color. And there was a new chair in the empty living room and their father had guessed they needed some paintings for the walls since they looked pretty bare and Patty had nodded and smiled and he had set up his easel. He had gotten one or two ideas after he saw Tommy's chain, he said, but in three days he finished seven seascapes—with lots of green and lots of silver—four for their walls, three for the Plymouth Fall Festival. One of them had two suns. "Just a crazy idea," said Tommy's father.

Tommy smiled. They weren't thrimble, he thought—but pretty close.

They *were* illil.

On Saturday, Tommy's father bought the pale yellow paint. He did the close brushwork around all the edges in the hall while Tommy watched, fingering the warm chain. Walls are supposed to be flat, but this was an old house and Tommy could see this wall wasn't even close to flat. It leaned in a little bit at the top and leaned out a little bit at the bottom. And there were ten, twenty, a hundred places where the wall bumped up, a thousand places where it nicked in. And Tommy had never noticed before, but there was a curve to it. If he looked with his head cocked to one side, the wall had a horizon.

His father poured the pale yellow paint into a pan and gave Tommy a roller to finish the hall while he went into the kitchen to see what could be done about the ruined cabinets. Tommy stepped back and looked at the bumps and nicks arranging themselves together across the horizon. He thought he might . . . Well, he wasn't sure what he might do.

But the chain was very warm.

He ran the roller into the pan with the pale yellow paint.

He looked at the wall again.

Then he began to roll the paint across the hallway wall. He finished quickly so that the whole hall was a pale yellow.

Then he began again—his chain was almost hot. He felt the way the wall curved, its bumps, its nicks. He pushed harder on the roller, lighter, then along the roller's edges, quickly, slowly, and then barely touching at all—the lightest whisper of pale yellow paint.

When Patty came out into the hall—she'd been sorting all the books that hadn't been stained green back onto the shelves their father had put up again—she looked at the pale yellow walls. She squinted a little, then tilted her head, then leaned back. Then she smiled, smiled, smiled.

"Do you like it?"

Patty put her arms around Tommy's waist.

Their father glanced into the hall as he was carrying out the last box of shattered dishware.

It was a good thing that it was only shattered dishware in the box.

"Tommy," he said. He squinted a little, then tilted his head. "Tommy, how did you do this?"

"I remembered," said Tommy.

His father put his hand to his face. He reached up and almost touched the wall. Then he stood back. "You remembered," he whispered.

He went outside. Tommy and Patty followed him.

They sat on the dune, a surprisingly warm breeze coming up from the sea. The long grasses were bobbing back and forth to each other, carrying the day's news as they do. Quiet seagulls hove to, their faces in the breeze, their eyes half closed, dropping down suddenly onto the planet when it suited them. Some jellyfish washed up and shimmering eerily beyond the sea reach. The salty wind. The cool, clean damp everywhere.

And on the sandy dune, the three Peppers sitting close, crying a little—a good crying. Remembering the way she held her head, the way she moved her hands, how easily she cried, how easily she laughed.

And inside, in the hall, pictures of Tommy Pepper's mother in pale yellow hints on pale yellow walls.

Thrimble and illil.

It hardly seemed that anyone in Plymouth should have been in the mood for the Plymouth Fall Festival. But as the farmers' market brought in yellow gourds and gallons of apple cider, and as the winds turned and the first frosts of the season laced the windowpanes, Plymouth felt that autumn would be lost if folks never had a chance to walk the 4-H stalls and smear cotton candy over their faces and cheer the tractor pulls and ride the Tilt-a-Whirl and eat footlong boiled hot dogs and elephant ears.

So on the last Saturday of October, Tommy and Patty and their father—who was carrying three of the sea-scapes—weren't the only ones who got to the fairgrounds early to watch the sows get their pre-judging milk baths, to see the great horses have their manes braided before the parades, to whistle as the giant pumpkins got weighed, to walk between the cages of the quick-eyed rabbits and the scatterbrained chickens and the white ducks with their startling orange bills. Everywhere there was the smell of sawdust and frying oil and good clean manure—except in the Big Tent, where the pies and jams scented the closed air with nutmeg and cinnamon—and everywhere the barkers were calling out, inviting them to try their luck on the Wheel of Chance, to have their fortunes read, to choose from among the Oriental glass beads brought back from deepest Asia, to win a giant panda by making three only three that's right just three baskets in a row, to see the one the only the original Cardiff Giant, the great-est hoax of all time!

They met Alice Winslow around ten o'clock and she hugged Patty and told her that she would braid her hair if she wanted and Patty nodded and they found a bench near to the Musical Stage and close enough to the food booths that they could get a hot elephant ear and watch the acts while Mr. Pepper went to the seascape painting exhibit. Mr. Pepper gave them a bunch of tokens and said they'd meet again right at noon, okay? By the apple pie booth? Patty would stay close to her brother? Promise? Good.

Alice Winslow and Tommy and Patty had eaten five elephant ears between them—which they figured was probably more than they should have—and heard the Foxboro Fiddlers perform with their star fiddler fiddling behind his back, and the Andrews Sisters Redux sing a medley of World War II top hits, before James Sullivan found them.

"Am I too late?" he said.

"For what?" said Tommy.

"Belknap."

They looked at him.

"Belknap is playing today."

"Playing what?" said Tommy.

"His accordion."

"In front of everyone?" said Alice Winslow.

"No, he's going to wait until everyone leaves," said James Sullivan.

"That might not be a bad idea," said Tommy.

Patty hit him on the shoulder.

"That's right," said James Sullivan. "Hit him again."

Patty might have hit him again if a guy wearing a gold-sequined coat hadn't come on stage and announced Pat Bellnip and His Sweet-Singing Toe-Stomping Dance-Making Accordion playing a Medley of American Folk Songs, and Patrick Belknap, wearing a black cowboy hat, stepped out onto the stage.

Alice Winslow said, "Oh my goodness."

They could tell he was nervous, slinging his accordion around. His eyes were blinking—a lot. And his cheeks were bright red. His mouth was open as if he was sucking air.

But then he started in on the Medley of American Folk Songs.

Tommy had to admit, he wasn't half bad. But the people around the stage thought Pat Bellnip and His Sweet-Singing Toe-Stomping Dance-Making Accordion were great. Some started stomping their toes, all right, and two couples got up close to the stage and began to dance, and then three couples, and then a whole lot more, and James Sullivan took Patty's two hands and started to dance with her, and then what could Tommy do when Alice Winslow pulled him up and said she didn't care if his hands were covered with cinnamon?

Tommy figured he'd have to punch Pat Bellnip in the face when this was all over.

Afterward, the Swampscott Barbershop Quartet took the stage, and Patrick Belknap climbed down and everyone clapped as he walked by—you could tell he liked that. He came over, and Alice Winslow told him he was great and James Sullivan and Tommy said he looked dumb in a cowboy hat. Patrick Belknap said he saw Pepper dancing with Alice Winslow and Tommy told him shut up and Alice Winslow asked why he hadn't told them he would be playing and he said would *they* say anything if *they* were going to get on stage at the Plymouth Fall Festival? James Sullivan and Tommy both said not in a million years, and then they all decided to get elephant ears— even Tommy and Patty and Alice Winslow again—and Tommy said at least the hat was great and Patrick Belknap lifted it off his head and put it on Tommy. "Yours for the morning," he said, and Tommy adjusted it so that it fit low over his eyes.

They bought the elephant ears and listened to the Swampscott Barbershop Quartet until they couldn't take it anymore and then they walked out to the Midway and they each placed a quarter on a spin and Alice Winslow won a fuzzy white koala bear and gave it to Patty, who held it close. Then they all stood at a bar and fired water pistols into a clown's mouth while the little ball rose on top of the clown's head and Tommy won— because of his cowboy hat, said James Sullivan. So they used five tokens to play again and James Sullivan wore the cowboy hat this time and he won and said "I told you so" and so Tommy fired his water pistol at James Sullivan and James Sullivan fired his at Tommy and the guy behind the bar hollered at them and Tommy took the cowboy hat back.

But Tommy was pretty wet, and maybe that was why, when a barker hollered that they only had to pay three tokens to see the Cardiff Giant the Greatest Hoax of All Time, Tommy suddenly felt very, very cold.

Even though his chain had suddenly warmed.

"Come in, come in," the barker called. He was a tall man, with shadows across his face. He wore a dark suit, and a dark shirt, and dark gloves. "Come in." He looked at them. "Come in."

They paid their tokens. They went into the tent.

Inside, the sawdust underfoot was worn down to furrows, and the sawdust in the air sifted through the shafts of sunlight the plastic tent windows let in. James Sullivan and Patrick Belknap and Alice Winslow and Tommy and Patty passed the poster displays—THE CAR-DIFF GIANT!!! THE PETRIFIED MAN!!! A GIANT OF EARLIER TIMES!!!—and then James Sullivan lifted the sheet that divided the outer tent from the inner tent.

The chain was hot.

"We shouldn't be here," said Tommy.

James Sullivan looked at him. "You scared, Pepper?"

Tommy was scared.

"No," he said.

James Sullivan ducked through. Then Patrick Belknap. Then Alice Winslow.

Patty took Tommy's hand, and they ducked in too. Tommy felt the dark close around them.

They were alone in the tent.

Tommy held Patty's hand tightly.

Another thick layer of sawdust on this side of the tent, also furrowed, and a long trestle table with a rope strung around it to keep people back. And lying on the table, what looked like a stone man, long arms tight at its sides, face eroded away so that it was blank except for a mouth, long legs slightly apart, and looking like it weighed more than any of the giant pumpkins Tommy had seen being weighed.

Maybe it was the thick sawdust, or being inside the tent, or the dark, but everything was very quiet.

"Look how tall it is," said James Sullivan. He was whispering.

Tommy felt the chain almost burn him.

Patrick Belknap leaned across the rope.

"Don't touch it," said Tommy.

Patrick Belknap looked at him. "It's made out of stone," he said slowly.

"Just don't touch it."

Patty tightened her hand in Tommy's.

"It's okay," said Patrick Belknap, and he reached over and grabbed the giant's foot. "It's not alive, Pepper. It's not going to move or anything."

Of course it wasn't going to move, thought Tommy. It was made of stone. It wasn't alive.

"People once thought it was real," said Alice Winslow.

"That's why it's called a hoax," said James Sullivan.

But it did look real, thought Tommy. Very real.

The feet were too large. They could almost have been webbed. The legs had knees that came too low. The torso and chest were too thin, too long. The left hand hung down almost to its low knees. And its head was too large, and—

"Wouldn't this look great in Mr. Burroughs's room?" said James Sullivan.

Quickly, Tommy dropped Patty's hand and went around to the other side of the stone man.

"The William Bradford Elementary School Giant," said Patrick Belknap.

Tommy looked closely in the dark.

The right hand was missing.

"Hey, Tommy . . ." said Alice Winslow.

"Quiet."

They all looked at Tommy.

"Don't say anything else."

James Sullivan started to laugh. "Pepper, are you spooked?"

"We have to go meet our father," said Tommy. He came back around and took Patty's hand again.

"Pepper, what are you doing?"

Tommy took Patty out of the dark.

"Hey, Tommy. Hey, wait."

But they didn't wait.

They left the tent, and the shadowed barker—who was no longer hollering—watched them pass.

They met their father at the apple pie booth, but Tommy didn't want any of the apple pie he'd bought. His father said maybe he'd eaten too many elephant ears?

Tommy said this was important and he should come with them to the Cardiff Giant tent and his father said he'd sold all three seascapes and Tommy said this was really, really important so could he come with them?

And his father looked at him and he dropped the apple pie on a bench and he took Patty's hand. "Lead the way."

So Tommy did, and when they got to the Cardiff Giant tent, the barker was gone.

"The tent's closed," said their father.

Tommy went in anyway.

His father and Patty came in behind him.

Tommy pulled up the sheet.

There was nothing on the trestle table.

"There's nothing here," said Tommy's father.

But Patty pulled on his arm and her father looked down at her. Then he looked at Tommy.

"It was the O'Mondim," said Tommy.

Their father drew Patty to him. "We'd better go home," he said.

Tommy and Patty nodded.

They left without even giving Patrick Belknap his cowboy hat back.

That night was the coldest yet, and cloudy. Before he went up to his loft, Tommy—with Patty and their father—watched the sea from the front windows, but without the moonlight, they could barely see the whitecaps breaking.

After he went up to his loft, Tommy watched the sea from his dormer window. Still, only the breaking white-caps. And nothing interrupted their rhythm.

In the morning, when they went out to do the dawn, they watched the sea from the top of the dune. Everything was quiet, and the chain stayed cold.

All day, everything was quiet, and the chain stayed cold.

That night, everything was quiet, and the chain stayed cold.

On Monday, Tommy held Patty's hand when they got on the bus, and if Cheryl Lynn Lumpkin even looked his way, he began to take his glove off—and she looked somewhere else. Mostly she looked at the houses along the coast, which is where everyone else on the bus was looking, wondering if any of those houses had been broken into overnight. Wondering when their own houses might be broken into.

Tommy didn't think they needed to worry. He knew, somehow he knew, that there was no more need for the break-ins.

But they watched anyway, driving under the maples getting ready to shake down their last curling red leaves.

And then, once again, everyone on the bus had even more to wonder about.

There was the first police car that sirened out from behind the bus, lights flashing, wailing.

There was the second police car that turned onto Water Street barely a block ahead of them and went after the first, wailing just as loudly.

And then the third and fourth—Massachusetts state troopers this time—cutting in front of the bus, blue lights eerie in the early light.

When the bus got to William Bradford Elementary, all four police cars were twirling their lights in the parking lot. Mr. Zwerger and Mr. Burroughs were standing out front, watching the buses come in and pointing them all toward the first grade side.

Except Tommy's bus.

When Mr. Zwerger read their bus number, he said something to Mr. Burroughs, and then he went to talk to the gathered policemen.

Mr. Burroughs walked over to the bus, waved at Mr. Glenn, and came on. He looked across the rows of seats and finally saw Tommy. He walked down the aisle and leaned toward him.

"Tommy," he said, "something's happened."

Tommy felt Patty's hand grip his.

"I've called your father. He's coming right away."

It wasn't Mr. Burroughs's fault that Tommy had heard those same words once before. And that Patty had heard them too.

Tommy thought he was going to throw up.

"I want you to come with me," said Mr. Burroughs.

They had heard those words too.

Patty held on to Tommy's hand. She wasn't going to let go.

"Both of you," Mr. Burroughs said. "Miss Minerva is waiting for you in the main office, Patty. Your father will come there first to pick you up."

Tommy and Patty gathered their backpacks and followed Mr. Burroughs off the bus. No one spoke. But everyone on the bus watched. And every policeman in the parking lot watched while Tommy and Patty walked across the parking lot and into the school. And every teacher in the halls of William Bradford Elementary watched while they walked down the first grade hall to the main office. And there, everyone in the office watched while Miss Minerva came to take Patty's hand. Tommy didn't want to leave her, but Patty nodded to him. She would be okay.

On the way down the hall to their classroom, Mr. Burroughs watched Tommy. "Listen, Tommy," he said. "There isn't anything you want to tell me, is there?"

Tommy looked up at him. "Like what?"

"Like how you can cut a cake like no one has ever cut a cake before. Like how you can make a drawing that seems to move. Like how you suddenly think there are two suns in the sky."

"There's only one sun in the sky."

"And, Tommy, is there someone who wants something you have?"

"Something I have?"

Mr. Burroughs nodded.

Tommy thought. "Mrs. Lumpkin," he said, finally.

"Mrs. Lumpkin?"

"She wants our house."

Mr. Burroughs shook his head. "I don't think this is Mrs. Lumpkin."

"Is there anything you want to tell *me*?" said Tommy.

"See for yourself," said Mr. Burroughs, and they walked into the classroom. They didn't have to open the door—Tommy thought this was pretty familiar—because the door had already been torn off, broken in two, and thrown down the hall.

It was probably the only thing in the classroom that was in two pieces—everything else was in a whole lot more. Every chair, splintered. Every desk, smashed. Mr. Burroughs's desk, smithereens. The whiteboard, shattered. The books, shredded. The shelves they had been on, pulverized. If a hurricane had roared into Mr. Burroughs's classroom overnight, it couldn't have looked any worse.

And the fah smell! Something stank as though it had been dragged up from the bottom of the sea. Like rotten seaweed, only more rotten than any seaweed that had ever rotted before.

The chain warmed.

The smell in the room, the fah smell, was the smell of hate.

The smell of the Field of Sorg Cynnes on the day the O'Mondim overwhelmed the battlements at Brogum Sorg Cynna, when Elder Waeglim held to the last and perished under the trunco of the O'Mondim, when Bruleath of the Ethelim stood in his place and rallied the Valorim against the Faceless Ones. The stench of their defeat lingered in the air through many risings of the Twin Suns, and the Valorim were avenged on that field, but the hanoraho did not blow at the settings of the Suns, or their risings. And the O'Mondim had vowed dark vengeance upon the Valorim, and upon those who stood under the shelter of their Art.

"Tommy?" said Mr. Burroughs.

And Tommy was afraid, deep down.

Mr. Burroughs took a step toward him. "Tommy, are you all right?"

And then Tommy looked at the wall of the classroom, written on with a black marker before all the markers had been snapped in three pieces, and he saw these words:

PEPPER GIVE US WHAT WE WANT

"This isn't Mrs. Lumpkin," said Mr. Burroughs.

Tommy nodded.

When his father got to the classroom, holding Patty beside him, he didn't think it was Mrs. Lumpkin either.

"Any ideas about what they want?" said one of the policemen.

"None at all," said Tommy's father.

"You kids got any?"

Tommy and Patty shook their heads.

The policeman put his hands on his hips. "Someone

who's pretty good at breaking things up knows your name," he said, "and they know what school you go to. I guess they probably know where you live."

"I'd say so," said Tommy's father, looking around.

"And they think you have something they want."

"They're wrong," said Tommy's father.

"It doesn't much matter," said the policeman.

It was Mr. Zwerger who suggested Mr. Pepper take Tommy and Patty home, and the policemen said they'd send a patrol car along with them—just to be sure everything was okay back at the house.

Mr. Zwerger said maybe they should take a couple of days. Maybe even take the rest of the week. Until things got cleared up.

It seemed to Tommy that Mr. Zwerger wasn't too eager to have them in William Bradford Elementary School.

Mr. Pepper went into the main office with the principal to sign them out while Tommy and Patty waited in the hall. And when they were alone, Patty reached up to her brother's chest to feel the chain through his shirt.

"I think so too," he whispered.

She yanked it once.

"I can't give it to Dad," Tommy said.

She looked at him, waited.

"Because it's harder and harder to remember her,"

he said. "I can hardly remember her voice. Sometimes I can't remember her face. Or her . . . But with this . . ."

He couldn't finish. Tommy Pepper tried not to cry outside the main office of William Bradford Elementary School.

Until Patty put her arms around him.

ELEVEN

Hileath

It came to the heart of Remlin that he might betray the Lord Mondus, and so save himself from what he knew was most certain. And it came to him that he might stand with Young Waeglim. So it was that Remlin left the Seats of the Reced and brought one of the O'Mondim with him, and he had the ykrat unknotted and the door opened, and he entered into the black hollow cell of Young Waeglim.

It might have come that Young Waeglim would have allied himself with Remlin. But that is a story never to be told. For when the door opened, Young Waeglim's mood was glad, and he sprang with the strength of twelve upon him, and tore the orlu from the hand of Remlin. And neither Remlin nor the O'Mondim with him ascended from that cell.

But Young Waeglim did ascend, wearing the robes

of a Councilman who sat in the Seats of the Reced, blinking against the hard light with downcast eyes, and when his back was to the Reced and no alarm sounded, he looked up, and marveled at what the City of the Ethelim had become in its rucca ruin.

Everywhere was desolation. The wind blew across the pedestals where once had stood the forms of Harneuf, and of Githil, and of Elder Waeglim himself. The gliteloit of the shops were all shattered, their shards still in the streets. All light was blackened out. Even the great crystal columns of the Hall of the Valorim lay upon the ground.

The air was unfere, rucca with the odor of O'Mondim filth, and Young Waeglim wept, and he did not hide his tears, for such tears cannot be hidden. He kept his hand on the orlu of Remlin, and if one of the O'Mondim had come his way then, grievous would have been his fate, and quick.

In his tears, Young Waeglim did desire, more than his life, that the Art of the Valorim would come back to this world, for now that he was free, the Art could do much to rebuild what the O'Mondim and the faithless Valorim had cast down.

Then did Hileath, daughter of Bruleath, come upon Young Waeglim, and at first her heart was hardened, for she thought he was a Councilman. But as she watched, often he fell against the side of a ruin as one who knew hunger for an old friend—as did all the Ethelim now. So when he fell and did not get up, her heart rose, and she went to him, and when he opened his eyes to her, she saw they were pale, and she knew him as one of the Valorim. She was amazed, for she thought that the Valorim were all gone from this world.

"You must rise," she said. "It will not be long before they come."

But she was too late. Far down the ethelrad, four of the O'Mondim came, trunco drawn.

And Hileath remembered the tales of her father, Bruleath, of the kindness of the Valorim. She remembered the nights when Elder Waeglim had told her the tales of her father's bravery, of how her father had saved the life of Elder Waeglim at Sorg Cynnes, and of how they stood together as brothers, resolving to battle side by side, and to win or perish, together. She remembered how Elder Waeglim had given his life at Brogum Sorg Cynna to save the Ethelim.

Hileath spoke. "The O'Mondim will come upon us," she said.

She saw him grip his orlu. She knew that he would not flee.

Young Waeglim took the life of the first before the O'Mondim knew an enemy was upon him. The O'Mondim's trunc fell to Hileath, who grasped it hot from the O'Mondim's hold.

The second O'Mondim had only the time to cry out before his long body too fell bereft of soul—if souls hide in the bodies of the O'Mondim.

But the other two set upon Young Waeglim with mighty blows, and Young Waeglim was sorely weakened. The trunco flashed down upon him with cold clanging, and his arms and shoulders were bloodied, and he was driven back upon the shattered glite, and fell.

Then did Hileath, daughter of Bruleath, remember again the tales of her father, and she came upon the O'Mondim, and they fled from her onslaught. And Hileath spoke to Young Waeglim. "Now is the time to remember the days of the Valorim. Now is the time for sure hearts, for keen orluo, for glory in battle."

And Young Waeglim, hearing Hileath, rose, and they stood together, resolving to battle side by side, and to win or perish, together. And the O'Mondim drew upon them again, and with a cry did Young Waeglim slaughter the first of the O'Mondim, and took the life from him. But Hileath was sorely pressed, for with a blow, the O'Mondim did shatter the trunc of Hileath. Then did the O'Mondim rejoice—but not for long. For Hileath threw herself against him, and when he fell, his hand opened, and his trunc fell to the street.

Hileath found it, and the O'Mondim never rose again.

Then did Young Waeglim let himself be led, and they staggered upon the ethelrad until they came to the house of Bruleath, who first saw his daughter, and then the pale eyes of the Valore, and Bruleath saw in those eyes the eyes of his friend, Elder Waeglim.

That night, the green alder from the Valley of Wyssiel that Bruleath had kept so long was opened, and there was rejoicing in the house. But they let no light shine, and their cheer was quiet, for the O'Mondim were in the streets, and Young Waeglim knew that they would never stop their hunting for him.

TWELVE

The Fah Smell of Seaweed

At seven thirty, on the Tuesday after the Fall Festival, in the Assembly Room of the Plymouth town offices, the Plymouth Planning Commission held its hearing on the request for an easement across the property of Peter R. Pepper for the purpose of building the PilgrimWay Condominiums, the request coming from Lumpkin and Associates Realtors of Plymouth, Massachusetts.

Tommy, Patty, and their father were there.

Mrs. Lumpkin was there too—and her associates, and her lawyers, and her lieutenant governor husband, who all rose to give their reports to the Plymouth Planning Commission.

Reports that cited the approval of almost all the neighbors whose property abutted the proposed easement.

Reports that said that Lumpkin and Associates Realtors would be glad to bear the cost of the new infrastructure to carry any additional traffic.

Reports that said that the building and maintenance of PilgrimWay Condominiums would bring a substantial number of both immediate and long-term jobs to Plymouth.

Reports that promised cutting-edge, environmentally friendly building techniques.

Reports that promised increased income for local businesses.

Reports, reports, reports.

Then the Planning Commission asked if Mr. Pepper had anything to say.

He stood. But he couldn't even speak. Tommy saw him searching, searching for words, but what could he say against the tidal wave of reports sweeping over them all, leaving Mrs. Lumpkin grinning? He shook his head.

Tommy's chain warmed.

His father was about to sit down.

Mrs. Lumpkin was really grinning.

And Tommy stood and took his father's hand.

The chain was hot.

His father did not sit down.

Tommy's father talked about Plymouth. He talked about a cold, bleak, gray November day when people who had suffered a long ocean voyage came to the shore to find a new way of life. He talked about what they saw when they stood on that coast and looked out to sea, and then looked inland. And he talked about how maybe, just maybe, some part of that shore should be kept as it once was, as those early Plymouth settlers first saw it, as Native American tribes had seen it for uncounted generations before that. Maybe, just maybe, not every single bit of it needed to be sold off and built up.

He talked about the shoreline, about the clean ocean smell, about families walking along the ocean's edge and picking up what the waves were tossing to them. He talked about loading pockets with perfect white stones. He talked about seagulls tussling on the wind, about the sound of the tide coming in, about the moon on the tips of the waves, about the sun lighting the horizon. He talked about what it felt like to stand on the coast and feel all America behind him.

Then he sat down.

Tommy watched the Planning Commission when his father had finished, and he knew they had all gone back to some day when they too had walked along a beach, filling their pockets with white stones while the tide ran out.

If they had taken the vote right then, Tommy was sure the PilgrimWay Condominiums would have blown away in the sea breeze.

But they didn't.

Mrs. Lumpkin stood up. She had never heard such claptrap in all her life, she said. Not in all her life. Her family went back to the *Mayflower,* for heaven's sakes. To the *Mayflower*! Who was Peter Pepper to lecture a *Mayflower* descendant?

But she had one or two more reports that she would like to present to the Planning Commission. Would they mind terribly a one-month delay? Just four weeks?

The Planning Commission, still in their dream of the shoreline, nodded approval of the delay, and Mrs. Lumpkin and her lieutenant governor husband—not very satisfied—left.

The Peppers walked home, Tommy and Patty holding their father's hands.

"Another month," said their father, "is another month."

That night, the waves rumbled, broken and shattered, high up the shoreline by the Peppers' house. Tommy lay awake listening to them, wondering if they would wash away the yellow flags—again. And by the sound of them, they might. They crashed one after another, and Tommy imagined their fierce falls into each other and the terrible drag of them as they pulled back into the seabed. One after another, after another, after another, the wind sweeping up their backs.

Tommy got up and went out into the hall, where the

table lamp flickered with sudden gusts. His mother's image on the pale yellow wall moved beside him in the glow.

By the front door, Patty was already waiting for him, holding both their coats.

"You should be asleep," Tommy said.

She put on her coat.

He took her hand and they went out and sat down on the stoop, the wind fierce in their faces.

Never had Tommy or Patty seen the waves in such agony. They wrenched themselves out of the sea, they smashed, they battered. Meanwhile, the wind scudded the dark clouds barely overhead, and the moon—which should have been full—was blotted out.

"Patty," said Tommy after a long time, "you really should go back to bed."

She scrunched in closer to him.

He held her and they watched together. They watched until their father came out, went back in, and came out again with the wool blankets, which he draped around the three of them. They watched side by side until the wind dropped a sudden icy rain.

It was late, but they decided to build a fire in the fireplace anyway to drive away the chill. And the flames came up quickly, the crackling of the pine kindling louder even than the falling rain, and Patty and Tommy sat close in with the woolen blankets still around them—while their father went down to the cellar to fetch some bigger oak splits.

And suddenly, with a lurch, Tommy felt the chain pull at him. He was sure of it. It pulled at him, back away from the fire. "Patty," Tommy said.

She looked up. The wind rising again. The rain louder, again, than the fire.

"Patty, let's get up on the couch."

They did, and they had not even put the blankets over their legs when a new gust of wind swept, battered, bolted its way down the chimney and, as if it knew what it was doing, scattered the red-glowing embers out into the room where they had been a moment before, and blew the fire into oblivion.

A scream—maybe the wind—came from the beach.

Tommy jumped off the couch and grabbed the shovel by the hearth. Quickly he scooped up the bright embers and threw them back into the fireplace, but the smell told him that they would find some burns in the rug come morning. He scraped across the braids with the shovel once more, then felt for any hot spots.

Patty held out both her hands.

"It's only the wind," Tommy said. "It's nothing to be . . ."

She shook her hands at him.

Tommy put the shovel back on the hearth and sat down next to her. She scooted to him as close as she could and buried her face against his side. He wrapped the blankets around them.

Another scream from the beach—Patty shuddered—and the still glowing embers burned brighter with the wind that swept down through the chimney.

Finally, finally, their father came back in. "That wind is really strong tonight," he said, holding the new splits. "And the sound of it! It's almost as if something is out there."

Then something pushed at the front door.

Tommy's chain pulled again. And again.

Another push at the front door.

Their father looked at them. "*Is* something out there?"

"Don't open it," said Tommy.

Patty shook her head.

Their father looked back at the door.

Another push. And again, the wind so loud that the sound itself seemed to be wrenching the old clapboards from the house.

The chain was hot.

Quickly Tommy got down by the hearth—the embers were still glowing. He grabbed two sticks of pine kindling and three of the splits and shoved the embers close together—another push at the door—and then he gathered the thinnest of the kindling around the glow. He knelt low and blew. And blew. And blew.

His father went to the door and listened, his hand on the knob.

Patty came and knelt beside Tommy, the blanket over her shoulders.

The door pushed again.

Tommy gripped the chain, hot as it was. Then he and Patty blew together. And blew.

A tiny flame. A tiny red flame along the underside of the kindling. Tommy blew against it carefully.

The wind shrieked down the chimney again.

The tiny flame went out.

Another push at the door, but this time, the wind—was it the wind?—pounded against it, pounded and pounded.

Tommy's father came back into the living room and gathered Patty to him. "What in the world is happening?" he whispered.

The fah smell of rotten seaweed.

Tommy felt the chain pull him down, down, down to the hearth. And then, he felt it leap.

And the pine kindling burst into hot blue flames.

The wind shrieked down the chimney again, but Tommy added more and more pine, and more, and then the oak splits.

Another push at the door.

More dry splits, and the flames higher. Then higher.

Quiet.

Then more quiet. The fire glowed brightly.

Silence at the door.

The storm blew on and on into the night, and sometimes the wind still rose to a terrible, terrible scream, as if the air were ripping, so that their father said, "It sounds like something dying."

But Tommy shook his head. "Something angry," he said.

They watched the fire for a long time. And when Patty had fallen asleep, Tommy's father said, "Tommy, tell me again about the O'Mondims."

"There's only one," he said. "And I think he's out there."

They stayed together in the living room that night. They never let the fire die down.

On Friday, their father drove Tommy and Patty to William Bradford Elementary School, and when they got there, it seemed that everything was pretty much the way it had been—except Officer Goodspeed was stationed outside the sixth grade door. They stopped in the main office to let Mr. Zwerger know they were back, and then Tommy headed to his locker. Everyone he passed watched him as though something was about to happen.

Tommy thought they might be right.

While Tommy had been away, Mr. Zwerger had gone downstairs to the school basement—where no one ever went—and brought up a huge, sprawling desk for Mr. Burroughs that was only missing one drawer. And he had found old desks for everyone else—old enough to have cut-out circles for inkwells in their corners. The desks still smelled of school basement, and even though all the windows were pushed up and there was new paint and a warm breeze and the classroom door was open because there was no new classroom door yet, the room still had the tang of rotten seaweed.

Other than that, everything else was pretty much the way it had been.

Tommy sat down. James Sullivan thumped him on the back with his not–Tom Brady–signed football. Alice Winslow told him that he was a cad for missing four days. ("A cad?" said Tommy.) Patrick Belknap reminded him that he still had his black cowboy hat. And Tommy told him he should come over to his house after school and maybe they could all come and they could play some football on the beach, because how many more warm days were there going to be? Then Mr. Burroughs came in and he asked Tommy how he was doing. Tommy said he was fine. When Mr. Burroughs said he looked tired, Tommy almost said that Mr. Burroughs would look tired too if he was up watching for an O'Mondim all night—but he didn't.

The warm breeze held through school and on into the afternoon, and the warm breeze was still blowing when James Sullivan and Patrick Belknap and Alice Winslow got to Tommy's house, and Patrick Belknap put on his black cowboy hat again and Mr. Pepper fed them chips and salsa. And the warm breeze was still blowing when they headed down toward the beach.

"Pepper!"

James Sullivan could only wait so long before he needed to throw his not–Tom Brady–signed football.

"Go long. Way long."

Tommy did. He ran up the beach and caught the way long pass—on his fingertips, again! Punted it to Sullivan. Then he caught another that James Sullivan threw hard into his gut because Patrick Belknap was guarding him. Punted it to Sullivan. Then another that Tommy had to stop and go back for, since Patrick Belknap was in James Sullivan's face. Punted it to Sullivan.

Then "Try this," and James Sullivan reared back and launched a pass that looked like it was going into the end zone. And Tommy ran, and then sprinted, and finally threw himself toward the ball, flat out over the sand—caught it with one outstretched hand—pulled it into his chest.

"Pep-per! Pep-per! Pep-per!" Patrick Belknap chanted.

Tommy stood up, mostly covered with damp sand.

James Sullivan was clapping. "Not bad," he was saying.

Then a sharp pang, and Tommy felt his chain twist and tighten. The football flew out of his hands and into the high waves.

"Hey," hollered James Sullivan. "Hey, that's my . . ."

The first white water slapped over the football and shoved it up toward the beach. Tommy ran down to catch it—it really wasn't so far out—but he wanted to keep his sneakers dry, so he looked up to see when the next wave was coming.

This is what he saw.

Twenty-five, thirty feet out, like a stone pier beneath the water, the O'Mondim stood, facing him.

Tommy reached for the halin at his belt, but it wasn't there.

"Get it, you jerk," called James Sullivan.

The retreating wave pulled the football farther out.

Tommy reached for the limnae behind his back. It wasn't there either.

"Pepper, what are you doing?"

Tommy watched the O'Mondim. Beneath the waves, the water and sand rushed and heaved, but the O'Mondim did not move. Even his faceless head did not move.

And Tommy Pepper was filled with a white hot hate. The O'Mondim, who had betrayed Hengel at Bawn and slaughtered the gentle Elil. The O'Mondim, who had overrun the battlements at Brogum Sorg Cynna to destroy what had taken the Valorim a thousand years to build. The O'Mondim, who . . .

"Pepper, thanks for nothing."

James Sullivan had rolled his jeans up to his knees.

"No!" Tommy hollered. "No! Eteth threafta!"

James Sullivan looked at him. "What?"

"Stay out of the water!"

James Sullivan shook his head. "That's my football in there."

Tommy grabbed him by the arm. He pointed to the waves. "Are you blind?"

"What?"

Tommy watched the unmoving O'Mondim beneath the water.

Patrick Belknap stood beside Tommy. "You see something out there?"

Tommy couldn't believe it. How could they not see him? He wasn't so far out. He wasn't even deep.

James Sullivan shook off Tommy's hand with the next wave and stepped into the water.

"Sullivan!" Tommy stepped in with him.

"Pepper, get off!" James Sullivan took another step into the water.

"Threafta! You jerk, threafta!"

But James Sullivan waded out. The O'Mondim did not move.

Tommy watched.

James Sullivan did not have to go far before the waves brought the football back in toward him, and when he finally grabbed it, he shook off the water and waded quickly back. "Was that such a problem?" he said.

Tommy watched.

James Sullivan shook the football. "If this is ruined, you owe me a football, Pepper. Again."

Tommy didn't say anything.

"Pepper!"

Out in the water, the O'Mondim raised his ruined right arm. It was hard to see, with the water swirling, but it looked as if . . . as if the O'Mondim was calling him in.

Tommy felt the chain warm, hot around his chest.

He shook his head. No.

"Pepper, what are you looking at?"

But the O'Mondim wasn't calling him in. He was pulling someone out from behind him, someone smaller, someone who was in the shadows under the water and half invisible, someone . . .

His mother.

Tommy took a step into the water.

She seemed to flow out from behind the O'Mondim.

Tommy took another step.

"Pepper?" said Patrick Belknap.

"What are you doing? I've got the football."

She was so pretty, her long black hair held back from the swirling water with the red kerchief.

Now the O'Mondim watched.

Tommy felt James Sullivan and Patrick Belknap grab hold of his arms. He shook them off like the maeglia they were. They grabbed him again, and he took two more steps into the water, dragging them with him. His mother moved toward him, almost as if she was coming out of the deep darkness, almost as if she knew he was close, almost as if . . .

He shook off the maeglia again.

Another step. The waves higher. Someone behind him yelling his head off.

The water up to his waist.

His mother let the cool water lift her arms up to him. He could hear her voice! "Tommy." He could see her face!

"Tommy."

Then, he felt something hard and heavy thud against him.

His eyes left his mother and he almost fell forward into the water. He turned, his hand up to the back of his head.

He did not see the football—the not–Tom Brady–signed football—caught by the next wave, dragged to the bottom, and then let up again.

"What was that for?"

James Sullivan and Patrick Belknap looked at him.

They were both standing in water past their knees, sopping wet.

"Get the football," said James Sullivan.

And then Patty came to the water's edge, dragging Alice Winslow by the hand.

She was crying.

"Patty," said Tommy, "Mom is . . ."

Patty let go of Alice Winslow's hand and she lifted her arms and held them out to him.

And Tommy took a step back out of the water.

Immediately the tide began to pull, ripping against his legs, holding the not–Tom Brady–signed football under the surface and dragging it out quickly.

"Tommy," hollered Alice Winslow. "Oh my goodness!"

But Tommy and James Sullivan and Patrick Belknap struggled out of the swirling water, and Tommy took Patty's hands, and she threw herself around him and sobbed.

Tommy looked back into the deep water. His mother, his mother, his mother was gone. The O'Mondim had moved farther out.

And his empty face was no longer looking toward Tommy.

He had turned to Patty.

And with hatred and loathing in his heart, Tommy cried out, "Byrgum barut! Su byrgum barut!"

The waves grew dark, and the O'Mondim was gone.

And Tommy's mother.

And the surf grew low and soft.

"I guess that's the last I'll ever see of that football," said James Sullivan.

Every school day now, Tommy's father drove them to William Bradford Elementary School. Each morning, Tommy and his father said to Patty, "Have a great day!" and they watched while Patty walked to the first grade door, and they waited for her to turn and wave.

"I will," Tommy whispered for her.

Then they drove around to the sixth grade door, where James Sullivan was always waiting for Tommy to go long and catch his throws on the ends of his fingers— except the throws were always messier than they should be because he had to use one of the William Bradford Elementary School footballs now, and they were short and stubby and beat up, and even Tom Brady couldn't have thrown a spiral with one of these.

But no one caught a football like Tommy Pepper, and James Sullivan kept heaving them out, just to watch them settle like homing pigeons into Pepper's hands.

At the first bell they would all go inside—the warm breezes were over, so they were always glad to go in—and they dropped their stuff off in their lockers and headed to Mr. Burroughs's classroom, where the smell of the new paint was fading, but the tang of the rotten seaweed was still holding on. Mr. Burroughs said that once they finished the solar system unit, they'd try some olfactory chemistry experiments to see if they could eradicate the stench. "And if you don't know what *olfactory* or *eradicate* means," he said, "here's a perfect opportunity to use our new classroom dictionary."

After Tommy was back for a couple of days, he could almost imagine the classroom was as it always had been, as if nothing had ever happened.

After Tommy was back for three days, he could almost imagine that even if something had happened, it was over and done.

After Tommy was back for four days, he figured even Mr. Burroughs had forgotten about what had happened in the classroom—everything was that normal. "Okay, let's try this again. Who can name the planets in order, starting with Mercury?"

A whole lot of hands went up. Alice Winslow named them all. In order.

"Right," said Mr. Burroughs. "Perfect. Now let's have everyone take out a sheet of paper—it's okay if it's lined, Jeremy—take out a sheet of paper and draw the planets in order, showing their relative size. Moons count too. You'll keep this for reference in your solar system folders—yes, Alice, I know there's a chart in *Science Today!*, but there's nothing like making your own."

Tommy drew all the planets in order. Showing their relative size. And their moons. As he worked, he kept his arm over the paper and drew thrimble, so that Jupiter's red spot churned across the planet, and Mercury spun wildly, and Mars's icecap glistened.

After Tommy was back for five days, the new old desks just felt . . . the same. And the classroom felt . . . the same. The perfect columns of desks were messed up, half of the new markers were uncapped, the rows of books that Mr. Burroughs had begged from the other classrooms were all out of order, and the whiteboard was stained from the markers that were supposed to wipe off easily but never did. And the smell of the paint was almost completely gone. It was as if it had all never happened.

Except for the rucca tang.

After Tommy was back for six days, his father let him and Patty ride the bus to school in the morning— but he still picked them up in the afternoon, since Tommy had to stay a little late so he and Alice Winslow could finish their sort of wobbly Styrofoam solar system project, which they were trying not to touch too much because of what would probably happen if they did.

And after Tommy was back for seven days, Officer Goodspeed left the sixth grade hall and resumed his double patrols around Plymouth. The break-ins had stopped, but Officer Goodspeed wasn't going to take any chances.

And during the days, Tommy fell into routines that were old and familiar: the dawns, the rides to school, Mr. Burroughs's classroom, catching footballs, the rides home along Water Street, homework on the solar system, supper, more homework on the solar system, reading with Patty. Sleeping.

Sleeping, sort of. Because at night, Tommy remembered the O'Mondim in the water, and he remembered his name on the ruined classroom's board, and his mother holding up her arms, calling his name. And he lay awake, and twisted his chain.

But in the mornings, he always walked into Mr. Burroughs's classroom sort of happy—he would never have told James Sullivan this—because they were talking about the solar system. And what could be more interesting than the solar system? When Mr. Burroughs drew the planets on the board according to scale, Tommy would draw them again in his notebook—always in thrimble to show they were revolving. And when Mr. Burroughs would start talking about Mercury's hot surface or Venus's poisonous atmosphere or Jupiter's red spot or Saturn's rings or Neptune's moons or about how small all of this was compared to the vast galaxy and how small our galaxy was compared to the vastness of other galaxies, Tommy would lean back in his chair and, for a little while, forget about the O'Mondim.

But Tommy was surprised at how much Mr. Burroughs left out.

Like how if you are living on a planet with binary suns, twice a year the tides are so high, the waves touch the clouds, so you can never build settlements near the shore—except for the hruntum that would wash away.

How you can feel the spin of a flat moon more and more as you walk toward its edge.

How the colors beyond Earth's short prism have sounds.

How light was only one way to measure speed. There was Thought, too. How else could you get to another galaxy?

And Mr. Burroughs didn't seem to know about the nebulae that hide behind the black holes and defy them with their own weird gravity.

Or why stars pulse.

Or what is at the center of a planet made of gases.

And if Mr. Burroughs thought the rings of Saturn were so special, hadn't he heard about the Ring Spheres around Alorn? He must have. Everyone had.

Tommy Pepper found it hard to understand why Mr. Burroughs left so much out.

Tommy figured he should try to be helpful. So when Mr. Burroughs said that it would take an astronaut longer than four years traveling at the speed of light to reach Alpha Centauri, Tommy raised his hand and pointed out it would only take half that many seconds on Thought, and Mr. Burroughs had raised an eyebrow and said, "Thought?" and Tommy said, "Yeah, Thought," and told him how light waves were tons slower than Thought waves. Mr. Burroughs had nodded his head and said yes, we can travel faster in our imaginations, and Tommy had smiled and said, "Exactly," and then Mr. Burroughs said they were in science class not science fiction class and everyone laughed and Tommy realized that Mr. Burroughs had not gotten it at all.

Tommy didn't try to be helpful again.

But Tommy really did like Mr. Burroughs.

So when on the day he was going to moderate a classroom debate on whether Pluto was a planet or not, Mr. Burroughs did not come in to William Bradford Elementary School, Tommy Pepper started to worry.

Mr. Burroughs had never missed a school day for as long as anyone could remember. Probably he had never missed a school day for his entire career.

But he did not come in.

And that morning, Tommy could hardly sit in his classroom, the fah smell of the O'Mondim was that strong.

THIRTEEN

Uprising

So the Lord Mondus sent the O'Mondim to hunt through the City of the Ethelim until Young Waeglim was found—alive, for the heart of the Lord Mondus still yearned for the Art of the Valorim, and he would not take Young Waeglim's life until the Chain was surely in his grip.

But Young Waeglim lay hidden in the house of Bruleath, and as the Twin Suns rose and fell, strength came back to his arms and light to his eyes and hope to his heart. And he said to Bruleath, "Now is the time to gather those who would fight for the side of the Valorim. Now is the time to remember old promises and the battles that were fought." And Bruleath sent word to those who had stood beside the Valorim in earlier days, and to their sons and daughters. And he gave to Young Waeglim the orlu and the halin that he had used when *he fought beside his father. And when Young Waeglim bound the orlu and the halin to his waist and across his shoulders, Bruleath drew back at the sight of him, so fierce did he look—and so much like Elder Waeglim in the battles they had fought together.*

They waited three days while the word went abroad and the O'Mondim searched the city. Behind the glite-loit, Young Waeglim watched with glowing eyes as the Valorim banes roamed the streets and spread their fah filth. He stored his anger in his heart, and with white hands he gripped the hilt of the orlu.

Finally, on a night lit only by a slanting of stars, Young Waeglim and Bruleath and Hileath and Ealgar left their home and headed to Brogum Sorg Cynna out-side the City of the Ethelim, where the O'Mondim would never come for the memory of the vengeance taken upon them. And there, the pale eyes of the Valore saw many of the Ethelim—though most weaponless. But in their eyes, Young Waeglim saw not hope but fear. And his heart was filled with pity for what they had endured.

"Is this what you have come to?" he said. "You who have fought side by side with the Valorim and taken the Reced and the city around it for your own? Is this the race that once drove the traitorous O'Mondim from the battlements, and with your own hands built

up all that is good and noble around you? Did the Valorim bring their Art into the world for this?"

But they murmured against him, and asked who he was to speak so. Had he lived in the city while it was torn by the O'Mondim? Had he been starved by their hands, been beaten by their hands, lost all by their hands? And now he comes, a lord of the Valorim, safe and well?

And Ealgar's anger was fired, and he stepped before them and spoke. He told of the Valore's long, dark suffering. He told of the battle with Hileath against the O'Mondim. He told of how Young Waeglim had sent the Art of the Valorim away from this world so that it might not fall to the hand of the Lord Mondus. And he told how Young Waeglim was the last of his race, and the power of their Art was gone from the world.

And they sorrowed for Young Waeglim and their misjudgment. They bowed the knee and swore they would fight with him against the Lord Mondus and the O'Mondim, as their fathers and mothers had fought before with Elder Waeglim.

And then Ealgar, son of Bruleath, youngest and smallest of all, who could not remember the days of Brogum Sorg Cynna, so young he was, said, "Where is the Art of the Valorim, that we might fight with it?"

And Young Waeglim said, "That you should be the

one to ask speaks most well of you." Young Waeglim put his hand on Ealgar's shoulder. "There is a way," he said, and his hand felt heavy to the boy, the heaviest thing he had ever carried.

And Young Waeglim told them what must be done to retrieve the Art of the Valorim. When he had finished, he asked if Ealgar could do such a thing. And Bruleath, the father of Ealgar, offered to do it in his son's place, but Young Waeglim said, "It is a task for the youngest and smallest, for the strength of one Valore alone is not the strength of the Valorim Ascendant, and the journey is as long as Thought."

And Ealgar felt his dreams come upon him. He remembered the stories of the Valorim. He remembered the stories of those who had fought with them. And his heart yearned to see again what the Silence had covered with dust and ash. So, with a voice that trembled not a little, Ealgar promised to do what Young Waeglim had spoken to them all.

And the eyes of the Valore looked again at the Ethelim, and this time, he saw hope.

Then did Young Waeglim gather the Ethelim into companies, and each company chose two to lead them, and each of the two came to Young Waeglim, and the Valore saw that their hearts were good and their minds keen and if their arms had not the strength that he might have hoped to bring against the O'Mondim, *still, good hearts and keen minds were nowhere among the Faceless.*

And what could there be against the Silence except battle?

And Bruleath, who had been sent by Verlim the Destroyer for a sign of the Ethelim's obedience, smiled grimly at the sign he would now carry back.

But he sat apart with his son, and with Hileath, and they trembled for what was to come. For how could anyone hope to leave this world, and come back?

Yet that is what Ealgar was to do.

FOURTEEN

Mr. Pilgrim Way

Tommy's class was wondering how long it would be before a teacher showed up. James Sullivan was betting the whole day, and he was already starting to push the desks to one side of the room to make an indoor football arena—even though they had only a stubby William Bradford Elementary School football to play with—when Mrs. MacReady appeared at the door, looking a little startled.

"Mr. Zwerger would like to see you in his office," she said to Tommy, and "Why are you pushing those desks that way?" to James Sullivan, and "I think I had better wait here until your substitute arrives," to the whole class. Everybody groaned. "I'm not paid to do this, you know." Everybody groaned again.

Tommy went to Mr. Zwerger's office. The fah smell of O'Mondim was so strong in the halls, he wondered how anyone could stand it. Or didn't they smell it? No one seemed to notice anything.

He walked into the main office, and since Mrs. Mac-Ready wasn't there to make him wait, he knocked on Mr. Zwerger's door. It opened immediately.

Mr. Zwerger looked a little startled too.

"Tommy Pepper," he said quickly, "thank you for coming." He almost pulled Tommy into the room, and taking him by the shoulders, he held Tommy between himself and the other man in his office.

The tall man. With shadows across his face. Wearing a dark suit, and a dark shirt, and dark gloves. He stared at Tommy. He was very still.

"Tommy Pepper, this is Mr. Pilgrim Way," said Mr. Zwerger.

Mr. Pilgrim Way stood, smiled.

"I think we've met," said Mr. Pilgrim Way, "in a way."

"He's been admiring your painting," said Mr. Zwerger. He pointed to the cottage.

Mr. Pilgrim Way nodded. "It is a very unusual"— Mr. Pilgrim Way paused, looked out the window, looked back at Tommy—"technique," he said. "That is, unusual for this place."

Tommy wished very much that Mr. Pilgrim Way had never seen the painting.

Mr. Zwerger still had his hands on Tommy's shoulders.

"Mr. PilgrimWay is going to substitute for Mr. Burroughs while he's gone, and Mr. PilgrimWay has asked if you would be his special helper as he gets to know the class. I told him you would be glad to."

Tommy stepped back—which was not easy since Mr. Zwerger stood so close behind him.

Mr. PilgrimWay looked down at Tommy's chest, where the chain was warming quickly.

"We'll get along well," said Mr. PilgrimWay.

"PilgrimWay is an unusual name," said Tommy. "That is, unusual for this place."

"Is it?" said Mr. PilgrimWay. He smiled. "I'm sure there's much that is . . . unusual . . . about us both."

Mr. Zwerger angled himself a little bit farther from Mr. PilgrimWay.

"So, Tommy," said Mr. Zwerger, "if you would get Mr. PilgrimWay's things—that briefcase right there—and I'll get this folder, and we'll all go down to the classroom."

Tommy picked up the briefcase. It was light, and he wondered if there was anything in it. Mr. PilgrimWay followed them out of the office, walking with almost no sound, just behind Tommy all the way.

When they reached the classroom, Mrs. MacReady was holding the stubby William Bradford Elementary School football and coaching all the desks back to their right rows.

James Sullivan was not looking happy.

"Mrs. MacReady?" said Mr. Zwerger.

"This is not what I am paid to do," said Mrs. Mac-Ready.

"And you're not paid to . . ."

Alice Winslow put her hand over James Sullivan's mouth.

"Class," said Mr. Zwerger—he looked over once at Mrs. MacReady, but she shook her head and held the football in front of her chest—"class, this is Mr. Pilgrim-Way. Mr. Burroughs is not available to teach today, and so Mr. PilgrimWay will be substituting. I think you'll all agree that PilgrimWay is a wonderful name for a teacher at William Bradford Elementary School. I know you will all like each other, and that you will all behave exactly as you would if Mr. Burroughs were here." Mr. Zwerger looked at Mr. PilgrimWay and handed him the manila folder he was carrying. "The classroom roster," he said.

Mr. PilgrimWay nodded and took the folder. He went to Mr. Burroughs's desk and sat down. He watched them all.

Mr. Zwerger, and Mrs. MacReady in front of him, could not have left much more quickly.

And when they were gone, Mr. PilgrimWay opened the folder, took out the roster, and tore it up into twelve pieces.

"I'll get to know your names . . ." he said.

His mouth barely opened.

". . . soon enough."

"Dang," whispered James Sullivan. His hands gripped an invisible football.

"Dang, dang," whispered Patrick Belknap.

Tommy nodded. "Dang, dang, dang," he said.

Even sitting down, Mr. PilgrimWay was the biggest substitute teacher Tommy had ever seen. He was probably the biggest substitute teacher anyone had ever seen.

He had shoulders that stuck straight out, and arms that fell from them to hands as large as platters. Big platters. He did not turn his head, but moved his face with his shoulders. His mouth was set and straight.

The shadows across his face covered his eyes.

But when Mr. PilgrimWay began to speak again, Tommy realized that it was his voice that was the most remarkable thing of all. How had he not noticed this in Mr. Zwerger's office? His voice was sweet and beautiful. When he spoke, he sounded as if he were singing. You couldn't help but listen to him. You couldn't help but wish he would keep on talking forever. When he asked Alice Winslow to stand and tell him her name—he didn't go in alphabetical order, but by order of nyssi—Alice Winslow looked as if she had fallen in love with him. When James Sullivan stood and said his name, he looked as if he would give Mr. PilgrimWay his Tom Brady–signed football if he still had it. And when Patrick Belknap stood up and said his name, he looked like Mr. PilgrimWay had handed him free box seats on the first baseline side for every Red Sox game for the rest of his life—a seat for him, and for his accordion, too.

Tommy Pepper knew that he would come up next in order of nyssi.

Mr. PilgrimWay's shadowed eyes looked at him.

"Tommy Pepper," said Mr. PilgrimWay.

He didn't sound like he was singing it.

"Tommy Pepper," he said again. "I know you."

Tommy didn't stand. He slid down in his seat.

Mr. PilgrimWay's shadowed eyes left Tommy and moved around the classroom. Slowly. "It is good to meet you all," he said. "Mr. Burroughs has told me you are one of his very finest classes. I'm sure that we'll get along well."

Tommy peered around. The way that everyone was looking at Mr. PilgrimWay, he was pretty sure they would.

"Open your mathematics textbook. There are fifteen problems to do on pages eighty-five through eighty-six. When you finish, bring your answers to my desk."

Tommy looked around again. No one was groaning. Why was no one groaning? He opened his math book and turned to Alice Winslow. "Don't you think he's creepy?" Tommy whispered.

"Who?" said Alice Winslow.

"Who? Mr. PilgrimWay."

Alice looked at him. "He has the most beautiful voice I've ever heard," she said.

"But didn't you . . ."

"Mr. Pepper," Mr. PilgrimWay said.

Tommy started in on the fifteen problems.

They took more than an hour.

No groaning at all. Not from anyone. No one asking for help. No one asking to go to the bathroom. No one begging for mercy. Not even James Sullivan.

They finished one by one and they went up to show Mr. PilgrimWay their work.

When Tommy went up, he kept Mr. Burroughs's desk between them. He did not look at Mr. PilgrimWay. He kept his eyes on his worksheet as Mr. PilgrimWay went over it with a red pencil.

Mr. PilgrimWay held the pencil as if he had never held one before in his life. He held it like an orlu, for heaven's sake.

Tommy's chain warmed.

"We'll be working on the solar system in the afternoon," said Mr. PilgrimWay to the class. "I hope the results will not be as disappointing as they were this morning."

Tommy's chain throbbed with heat.

Tommy brought his solar system folder with him to lunch but left his lunch box in his locker. To hide it. But this time, not from anyone in his class.

In the cafeteria he checked the hot lunch menu. Corn dogs. Good. No one ever finished a corn dog. Before he ate, he went through his folder and picked out all the pictures of revolving planets he had drawn. He crumpled them all together—he could feel their motion within his hands—and he threw them into the bottom of the garbage bin. He looked around. It wouldn't be long before they were covered with half-eaten corn dogs.

At recess after lunch, James Sullivan went to the gym for another football, but the football he brought back was even stubbier. Tommy couldn't catch a single one of James Sullivan's throws. It was as if his hands had turned to rocks. The passes bounced off them and onto the asphalt.

"Pepper," said James Sullivan, "are you paying attention?"

"Yes, I'm paying attention," said Tommy.

"You do remember how to catch a football, right?"

"I do remember how to catch a football, you jerk."

"So run a cross."

Tommy ran a cross. The ball came into his hands, and he dropped it. It bounced onto the asphalt.

"Maybe I should throw to Alice," said James Sullivan.

The day had turned cloudy and cold over the morning, as if winter was thinking of shaking itself out of its long sleep and really showing its stuff. The brittle fronds of the daylilies alongside the sixth grade door rustled drily. A few drops of rain pattered, cold as ice.

Everyone decided to come in from recess early.

Tommy was the last one in.

When they got back into Mr. Burroughs's classroom, Mr. PilgrimWay was twirling Tommy's lunch box in his hands. He looked at Tommy and smiled.

It took Tommy a minute to see that everything in the classroom had changed. Instead of the posters Mr. Burroughs had put up on the new bulletin boards—posters of the entire Red Sox teams of 2004 and 2007 wearing their World Series rings and signed by every member of the team, every single member!—new posters of the solar system covered half the boards.

And the desks were now set up in nyssi order, so Tommy's desk butted up against Mr. PilgrimWay's desk.

"Neat!" said James Sullivan.

He tucked his stubby William Bradford Elementary School football in and ran the rows until he got to his own desk, and he closed the window against the cold rain—which was now coming down in more than a few patters.

Tommy watched Alice Winslow walk to her desk. It was at the very back of the classroom.

Alice Winslow hated having her desk at the very back of the classroom.

Alice Winslow complained loudly if her desk was at the very back of the classroom.

But Alice Winslow sat down as happy as all get-out. She looked at Mr. PilgrimWay and smiled.

"Tommy Pepper," said Mr. PilgrimWay. He almost reached toward Tommy, then pulled his hand back. "Your desk," he said, "is here." He pointed to the desk beside his own and laid the lunch box upon it.

Tommy looked into the shadowed eyes.

He sat down.

Mr. PilgrimWay began to hand out large sheets of paper.

"To start off our study of the solar system," said Mr. PilgrimWay, "we're going to draw a place on a far, far distant planet. A place far out of your solar system. Perhaps a planet that is much warmer than your own cold world."

He looked down at Tommy.

"Use your imaginations and be as creative as you wish, but give it . . . credibility. Make it seem as if it could exist."

Everyone started to draw. Even James Sullivan, who hated to draw, started to draw.

Tommy felt his chain twist and pull. He looked up.

Mr. PilgrimWay's eyes were on his chest.

"You'd better begin," said Mr. PilgrimWay.

"I don't really draw," he said.

Mr. PilgrimWay put his hand up around his neck, as if he were fingering a chain. "I don't think that's true," he said.

Tommy picked up his pencil. His chain was very warm.

He drew the Reced, with its high tower and long glazed gliteloit. He drew it on a night when the pennants were snapping, and when Ecglaef himself, ancient Ecglaef, was sending his spectacular naeli into the air, high into the air, where they exploded into swirling whirls with a shock that tasted of the sea. The hanoraho were sounding and the rylim tides were over and a new season full of light and cool winds was upon the city. Tommy closed his eyes. The sea! The smell of the clean sea!

Tommy drew thrimble and the pennants began to move and faintly, faintly, the naeli hissed. He could almost forget that . . .

"Who's ready to tack their picture up?" said Mr. PilgrimWay. He stood by the empty boards, a box of tacks in his hand. "Patrick Belknap?"

Patrick stood, still bending over his desk to finish his last couple of stars. Then he brought his picture over to the bulletin boards and Mr. PilgrimWay handed him a tack.

"Beautiful," said Mr. PilgrimWay. He did not look at it.

"Alice Winslow?" he said.

Tommy watched as Mr. PilgrimWay called up Alice Winslow, then James Sullivan, then Jeremy Hereford, then everyone else in the classroom, one by one. And one by one, he handed each of them a tack. And one by one, they pinned their pictures to the bulletin boards. And Mr. PilgrimWay said "Beautiful" each time. But he didn't look at any of the pictures.

"You don't think this is creepy?" said Tommy to James Sullivan when he walked by.

"What?" said James Sullivan.

"Tommy, yours now," said Mr. PilgrimWay.

Tommy put his arm over his picture. "I didn't finish," he said.

"Great art may sometimes have an unfinished quality. Karfyer always left a corner of his work unfinished. Do you remember?"

Tommy did remember.

"I thought you might." Mr. PilgrimWay grinned.

Tommy Pepper did not grin.

"There's one more space on this bulletin board," said Mr. PilgrimWay. He pointed. All the pictures were in nyssi order. Only one spot remained at the top of the angle. "Bring it up," said Mr. PilgrimWay.

So Tommy lifted his arm and picked up his picture, and brought it to the bulletin board, and Mr. PilgrimWay took it.

"Ah, the old fool Ecglaef," he said, and he pinned the picture to the board.

Then he looked at Tommy. And Tommy felt those eyes move down to his chest, again.

"Go sit, Tommy," said Mr. PilgrimWay. And when he sat, Mr. PilgrimWay pointed to the bulletin board. "Class, I want you to look at Jeremy's picture. He's drawn colored balls that are hovering in the air."

"They're meant to be—" began Jeremy Hereford.

"In our imaginations, we can even create games for a new world, like Jeremy's." Mr. PilgrimWay walked over to the solar system projects and plucked the Styrofoam balls from Alice and Tommy's. "Sometimes, we can make what we imagine into reality."

He held the eight balls in his hands.

"But only if we have power," Mr. PilgrimWay said.

He tossed the Styrofoam balls into the air, and they hovered. They hovered! Then he began to move his hand around and around and the balls floated apart and circled the classroom over their heads, near the ceiling.

Tommy kept his eyes down.

"Power," Mr. PilgrimWay whispered.

And the Styrofoam balls began to circle faster.

"All Art is about power," said Mr. PilgrimWay. "There is no Art made without power, and there is no reason for Art to be made except for power. That is the way of things, no matter what world you live on."

The balls were circling so fast that they were hard to tell apart. Tommy heard them whirring above his head.

They whirred a long time.

"Good," said Mr. PilgrimWay. "Very good. Now it is time to go to your Music Appreciation class. Quickly. Not you, Tommy Pepper. You stay here."

They all stood, their eyes following the circling Styrofoam balls, and they bumped through the desks. Patrick Belknap clipped his accordion and sent it to the floor, but he didn't stop.

Tommy watched them go.

He was glad there still wasn't a door to close behind them.

And when they were alone, Mr. PilgrimWay turned back to him. "You have learned almost nothing," he said.

Tommy kept his eyes from the circling balls.

"What you wear is the Art of the Valorim, and it is so much more than a child's drawing. It is so much more than bringing an O'Mondim out of the sand."

"Where is the O'Mondim?" said Tommy.

"In the ocean, waiting on the word of his Valorim master."

"He wants to go home."

Mr. PilgrimWay walked closer to Tommy.

"What an O'Mondim wants means nothing. But you, Tommy Pepper. You have worn the Art of the

Valorim. You have seen another world. You have felt what the Art can do."

Far down the hall, music class began. Mrs. Low started to play.

"Give me the chain and I will show you so much more."

Mr. PilgrimWay held out his hand.

Mrs. Low was playing the Bach piece.

"I can show you nothing without the chain, Tommy Pepper."

His hand still out.

The Bach piece played from down the hall. And suddenly Tommy remembered his mother's voice: "Oh, Tommy, I love to hear you play. Especially the Bach. I want to cry when I hear you play the Bach." He remembered his mother's voice! "I want to cry because it's so beautiful."

He remembered.

Tommy stood. "You're wrong," he said. "Art is not about power."

Mr. PilgrimWay smiled. "It is always about power," he said. He lifted his hand, gripped it into a fist, and pointed at Tommy.

Immediately one of the Styrofoam balls left its orbit and glanced off Tommy's left knee—and the ball had become as hard as stone.

He fell to the floor.

"Isn't it?" said Mr. PilgrimWay.

The second smashed into the bookcase beside Tommy's head.

"Tommy Pepper, we are not enemies. You have a chain that has given you special powers. I know what those powers are. Let me show you."

Mr. PilgrimWay held out his hand again.

Tommy backed up behind his desk.

The third and fourth balls flashed in front of his face. He felt their breeze.

"This is pointless," said Mr. PilgrimWay.

The other four balls flew toward his chest.

And then the chain leaped. And Tommy felt . . . something.

He held up his hand.

The eight Styrofoam balls were all circling near the ceiling again.

They were . . . dancing. Dancing to the rhythms of the Bach piece. Moving up and down, slowly turning, dipping, all in concert.

They were dancing.

Mr. PilgrimWay was staring at him. Then he looked up and began to move his hand around and around again. But the balls did not change their dance.

Tommy gripped his chair and pulled himself to standing. "I've learned a lot," he said.

They watched the eight balls dancing.

Mr. PilgrimWay smiled. "More than I had thought." He pointed to Tommy's knee. "And you have taken your lesson like a Valorim. Perhaps we will learn to appreciate each other."

"Why shouldn't I tell everyone who you are?"

"Who am I, Tommy Pepper?"

"I don't know. You're the barker from the Fall Festival." He gripped the chain. "And you're from another world."

"Who would believe you?"

"You're with the O'Mondim."

"I am not *with* the O'Mondim. I am its master."

Tommy gripped the chain even harder. He felt . . . knowing . . . pass into him. "You betrayed the Valorim, and you betrayed the O'Mondim. You told them"—Tommy closed his eyes—"you told them to rebel and they would rule the world. And then"—he opened his eyes—"then you took away their names. And you took away their faces."

Mr. PilgrimWay smiled and bowed.

"That's what you do. You betray people. You betrayed them all."

Mr. PilgrimWay stood straight and tall.

"And you, Tommy Pepper, you betrayed your mother. And with that, you betrayed your father and your sister, who no longer speaks."

It was as if the eight balls had struck Tommy in the

gut. He sat down. Suddenly he could no longer remember her voice.

Mr. PilgrimWay came closer. "With the Art of the Valorim, I can do much, much more to help you remember her. But you must give the Art to me before I can show you how."

Tommy shook his head. "I can't trust you."

Mr. PilgrimWay leaned toward him. "Let us be good to each other, Tommy Pepper," he whispered. "We are the same."

The Bach piece was still playing sweetly down the hall.

Tommy met Patty at the first grade door that afternoon. He took her hand and they went out to the sidewalk to board their bus. He looked down toward Plymouth Harbor and the ocean beyond. He held the chain underneath his shirt.

Patty looked up at him.

"Nothing," he said. "I hurt my knee a little, that's all."

She squeezed his hand.

"Really, that's it. I'm all right."

But nothing was all right.

By the end of the week, Mr. Burroughs still had not come back and everyone seemed to have forgotten about him—except Tommy.

"Isn't Mr. PilgrimWay wonderful?" said Alice Winslow.

"He's terrific," said James Sullivan.

"The best," said Patrick Belknap.

Alice Winslow, James Sullivan, Patrick Belknap—even Cheryl Lynn Lumpkin!—walked around as if Mr. PilgrimWay was a gift from the skies.

And, Tommy thought, he was.

But not the way they thought he was.

And not a gift.

At recess, Tommy went to see Mr. Zwerger.

Mrs. MacReady told him that Mr. Zwerger was awfully busy.

Tommy said he would wait.

"Suit yourself," said Mrs. MacReady.

Tommy waited through the whole recess. The door to Mr. Zwerger's office never did open.

"It's time for you to go back to class," said Mrs. MacReady.

When he got back to his classroom, Mr. PilgrimWay was flipping through pages of *Madeline*.

"That was my mother's favorite book," said Tommy.

"Was it?" said Mr. PilgrimWay.

On Monday, Tommy went to see Mr. Zwerger at recess again.

"He's still awfully busy," said Mrs. MacReady.

Tommy sat down to wait.

When he got back to his classroom, Mr. PilgrimWay had changed the whiteboard to a pale yellow.

He smiled when Tommy came in. "You're not carrying your lunch box anymore," he said.

"I lost it," Tommy said.

"It's almost certainly hidden in your closet." Mr. PilgrimWay smiled again.

And Tommy almost flinched, because that was exactly where his lunch box was.

On Tuesday, Tommy went to see Mr. Zwerger at recess again.

"I don't think he'll have time to see you," said Mrs. MacReady.

When Tommy got back to his classroom, Mr. PilgrimWay asked him where he had been. "I never see you outside, Tommy Pepper," he said.

"Sometimes I go to the library," said Tommy.

Mr. PilgrimWay waved his hand in the air. "There's so much to learn, isn't there? So much to remember. But I don't think you'll learn what you want to learn there."

Mr. PilgrimWay dropped his hand, and Tommy smelled . . . he smelled her perfume. The perfume she always wore.

Mr. PilgrimWay smiled.

On Wednesday, Tommy went to see Mr. Zwerger at recess again.

Mrs. MacReady was not at her desk, and the door to Mr. Zwerger's office was open.

Tommy did not wait. Who knew when Mrs. MacReady would be back? He knocked at the door and went in.

The room smelled of rucca seaweed. The room *stank* of rucca seaweed. But all the windows were closed and Mr. Zwerger was sitting with his back to his desk, painting at his easel, trying to copy the cottage picture.

"Mr. Zwerger?" said Tommy.

Mr. Zwerger did not answer.

"Mr. Zwerger?" said Tommy again.

Mr. Zwerger turned around. "Who are you?" he said.

"Mr. Zwerger, I'm trying to find out what's happening with Mr. Burroughs."

"Who?" said Mr. Zwerger.

"Mr. Burroughs."

Mr. Zwerger held his paintbrush in midair. "I'm very busy," he said.

"Is Mr. Burroughs coming back to school soon?"

Mr. Zwerger turned to his easel and began to paint.

"Mr. Zwerger?"

No answer.

Tommy shivered, and left.

Tommy went to the library. He found a phone book

and wrote down Mr. Burroughs's phone number. He went back to the office.

Mrs. MacReady was sitting behind her desk.

"I need to make a call," Tommy said.

"Students are not allowed to make phone calls from the main office," she said.

"It's an emergency."

"Are you bleeding?" she said.

"No."

"Then it's not an emergency."

"It'll be really quick."

Mrs. MacReady thought for a moment. "Two minutes," she said, and pointed to the phone.

Tommy called Mr. Burroughs's number. He let it ring twelve times. Then he hung up and tried again in case he had dialed wrong. He let it ring fifteen times. Then he hung up.

"Recess is over," said Mrs. MacReady.

Tommy was afraid to go back to his classroom.

He thought he might start bawling like a first-grader.

FIFTEEN

Battle at the Reced

Second Sunrise, and the Short Dark of the year.

The rylim tides, and the time of the Leaping of the Waves by the shore.

In the dark room of the Seats of the Reced, the Lord Mondus waited for word of Young Waeglim. That none had come brought fear to his heart and anger to his hands. And smoldering too in the Lord Mondus's thoughts was the Councilman Ouslim, and whether he might find the Art of the Valorim, and how, when he returned, the Lord Mondus might take the Art of the Valorim and do away with Ouslim and his sly and dreaming lies.

The Lord Mondus went to his chambers, dark and empty.

So he did not see the two who walked slowly

toward the Reced in that early light. One wore the robes of a Councilman of the O'Mondim, and one was small and took two steps to the other's one. Both were hooded and both walked firm of purpose, so that the O'Mondim who felt their coming pulled back and bowed as they passed.

The two came to the doors of the Reced and there, for the first time, the small one hesitated—but only a moment. For the doors were opened to them by the O'Mondim guards, and they must enter. And when the doors closed behind them, they crossed the Courts of the Ethelim, and the Great Hall of the Reced—as it had been called in that time before the fah filth of the O'Mondim had spread—and they passed through narrow halls, and still narrower, until they came to the spiraling stairs that rose to the Seats of the Reced, upon which only servants walked. And there, more than a few of those servants drew back, afraid at the sight of a Councilman.

And so Young Waeglim and Ealgar climbed upward.

And upward.

And upward.

And in his heart, Young Waeglim hoped that none might be sitting in the Seats, that they might pass unchallenged to the Tower.

But deeper in his heart, Young Waeglim hoped that

the Lord Mondus might be waiting for them there, or any of the O'Mondim, for the heat of vengeance was flaming.

As for Ealgar, who had seen the Leaping of the Waves so few times, he walked as if in his dreams, wondering at what he saw around him, and wishing that he might have seen it in the high glory days of the Valorim Ascendant.

So they came to the top of the stairs and to the Seats of the Reced.

And there they did not find the Lord Mondus.

But they did find Fralim the Blind and Naelim the bane of Ecglaeth.

Young Waeglim let drop from his shoulders the robes of Remlin. Then Fralim spoke: "Who is . . . ?" Those were his last words.

But Naelim was mighty in arms and hard in spirit. He would not call for aid, but fell upon Young Waeglim himself. And the striking of their orluo was terrible, and the blue sparks that flew from the blades lit the Seats to the eyes of Ealgar.

Heavy were the blows of Young Waeglim, but heavier still were the blows of Naelim. More than once, Young Waeglim was forced to the tiles of the chamber, and thrown down so that the orlu of Naelim missed only a little—and sometimes, it did not miss. The heart *of Young Waeglim began to fail him, and it seemed that the triumph of the faithless Valorim and the O'Mondim might be complete.*

Then did Ealgar's dreams come upon him, and Ealgar gripped the gyldn his mother had given him, and he came to the two, when Young Waeglim was held to the floor by Naelim's knee, and Naelim had raised his orlu, and Young Waeglim saw the end of all things. And Ealgar took his gyldn in both his hands and drove it deep into the back of Naelim the bane of Ecglaeth, so that Naelim turned his eyes to Ealgar and did sweep his orlu toward him. But Ealgar was the quicker, and the blade passed over him.

And Young Waeglim felt his strength return with his anger, and his weakness flee as his despair faded. His hand gripped his orlu with its earlier strength, and battle was joined. Never had there been any like it in the Seats of the Reced. The blue sparks shone brightly, brightly, and flew against the gliteloit of the room, shattering them all, so that the eyes of the Lord Mondus opened in his room far below, and he called to Saphim the Cruel and to the O'Mondim guard, and together they rushed to the Seats of the Reced.

And there they found the two O'Mondim Councilmen, both ended, and the door to the Tower where lay the Forge of the Valorim, bolted strong.

The O'Mondim took up the Seat of Naelim and began to batter at the Tower door, pressed on by the fearful anger of the Lord Mondus. And the only sound in the Seats of the Reced was the battering of that door.

Until a new sound came.

The Lord Mondus walked toward a shattered glite and looked down.

The sound was of battle, far below.

The Reced was under siege.

The Ethelim had come.

SIXTEEN

Storms Again

On a Saturday late in November, Mrs. Lumpkin drove to the Peppers' house again. Tommy heard her yellow Mazda honking from the bottom of the dune. When he opened the door, she waved for him to come down, and he went back in to get his coat since it was starting to snow, and by the time he got down to her Mazda, she was waiting by the open trunk of the car, and she was a little . . . prickly.

"Unlike some people, I don't have all the time in the world," Mrs. Lumpkin said. She pointed. "Take this out of the car and bring it to your father."

Tommy took out the wrapped canvas. He knew what it was.

"Tell him I never want to see it again," she said. "And tell him I'm not paying for it."

Tommy took it back up to the house and slid it into the front hall closet.

The snow swirled around the dune.

Everyone said they had never seen so much snow fall on the New England coast in November. At first they were gentle snows, covering everything with a deep and soft fleece. And the air was cold enough to keep the snow dry, so the flakes blew easily north along Water Street and down the beaches toward Tommy's house, where they passed through the field of yellow flags with not even a ripple.

But as the month went on, the squalls of snow grew heavier. In the mornings, the sky would darken as Tommy and Patty headed into school, so that by the time they reached the first grade door, the sky was almost black with clouds holding a whole lot of wet snow. By the time Tommy got inside the sixth grade door, the clouds were starting to split and splatter big wet globs of snow—not just flakes—onto William Bradford Elementary School. Then the day would get darker and darker, and snowier and snowier, until by the time school was finished, the buses were sloshing through hubcap-deep snow, wipers running frantically across windshields but not doing much good at all.

Finally, Mrs. MacReady persuaded a distracted Mr. Zwerger to cancel classes for the last week of November, since the storms seemed like they weren't going to give in, and the bus drivers weren't going to put up with snow past their hubcaps, and there was so much weight on the roof of William Bradford Elementary that Mrs. Mac-Ready wasn't sure the building would hold up and she preferred not to be in the main office when the ceiling came crashing down, thank you very much, because that was not what she was paid to do.

At home, the Peppers kept a fire going in their fireplace all the time. Mr. Pepper set up his easel and worked at canvases of stormy seas. Patty spread out on the rug, her books all around her. But Tommy watched through the front windows as the falling snow thickened and thickened into wild sheets that came up from the green ocean, whose waves he could see only when the wind took a deep breath before letting it out again and shrieking the snow toward the Peppers' house.

Tommy watched. It was just like the wind the faithless Valorim had called up at Brogum Sorg Cynna, before the battle, when they sent it screaming into the eyes of the Valorim with thundering from the clouds as loud as ten thousand trempo, so loud it had struck fear even into the hearts of the Valorim, and they had been driven back by the sudden onslaught of snow.

The fah O'Mondim.

Until Elder Waeglim had defied the O'Mondim. Elder Waeglim and his companion Bruleath. Bruleath of the

Ethelim. And with the Art of the Valorim, they had raised a wall of ice to turn back the O'Mondim, a wall that . . .

"I'm going outside," said Tommy.

Patty looked up.

"In this?" said his father.

Tommy put his coat on and warmed his hands one last time by the fireplace.

"I'll just go down toward the shore a ways."

His father stepped back from his canvas and cocked his head at the perspective. "You're sure, Tommy?" he said.

Tommy listened to the shrieking wind. The house shook with it.

"I'm sure. I won't be long," he said, and headed outside.

"Be careful, then," his father called.

Immediately, the snow was so thick, Tommy felt it pushing hard against his chest.

His chain felt very warm.

He ran down toward the beach, through the yellow flags—he might have trampled on two or three—and came to the water's edge. The waves were milky green and yellow, and they crashed through the snow so loudly that it was hard to know whether he was hearing thunder or the waves.

He backed up a few paces and began to gather the wet snow on the beach into blocks. They formed quickly and easily in his gloved hands, and when he pressed them, they turned into clear and hard ice. He set the first row all along the length of their land—the yellow flags gave him the boundaries. The waves pounded, and they almost reached up to him until he turned, pulled his chain out from under his shirt, held it out toward the water, and pushed the waves back.

He set the second row, and then the third—all clear ice. Each block gripping the others around it. But the wind so terrible that it drove up beneath his coat and he started to shiver so badly that his hands shook. He wondered if his eyeballs could freeze.

The fourth, fifth, and sixth rows done. Quickly.

Tommy came around to the other side of the wall so that his back was no longer to the waves. The wind followed and blew at his face and iced his breath.

The seventh row, up to his chest. The eighth.

His hands were freezing. He really, really wondered if his eyeballs could freeze.

He stood and looked back at his house. He thought, Elder Waeglim and Bruleath of the Ethelim at Brogum Sorg Cynna!

Quickly he set the ninth, then the tenth row in place.

Then he began the eleventh. The row that would raise the wall above his head. The thrygeth row.

He lifted the first clear block.

And the wind powered out of the sea and across the

beach. Tommy looked behind him. He could almost not believe that his house was still standing—but it was, the wood smoke streaming away from the chimney with the force of the terrible wind.

Tommy put the block in place. Through the clear ice, he saw the waves begin to roll like Chaos toward the wall, almost reaching it.

Quickly, another block, and then another, and another on the thrygeth row.

A wave galled itself against the wall, throwing its green foam upward.

Another block. Quickly, another block.

The waves fell back.

Another block. Another. And another.

The wind roared once, twice more. Again.

Then the wind stilled.

Another block. Another.

The wind held its breath, then let it out again, then held it.

Another block.

So quiet. The snow coming down softly now, in dry flakes.

Another block.

In the quiet, Tommy reached down, pressed his next block into ice, and set it in place. The eleventh row was done.

Thrygeth.

He took off his gloves, and with the chain, he carved into the wall the images of Elder Waeglim and Bruleath, standing shoulder to shoulder at Brogum Sorg Cynna, facing the O'Mondim storm in defiance.

And when he finished, Tommy looked behind him again toward his house. Except for one or two missing roof tiles, all seemed well. The wood smoke was rising straight up in the new calm. And the sun was suddenly there—hazy, but there—and the sounds of the waves had calmed to a quiet lapping. Tommy smiled, and he turned to look again at the sea.

But when he looked through his wall, he saw, on the other side of the clear ice, standing in his dark suit, his hands in his pockets, Mr. PilgrimWay.

Mr. PilgrimWay had never seemed so large.

They stared at each other through the ice.

"Tommy Pepper, you were not at Brogum Sorg Cynna," said Mr. PilgrimWay.

Tommy put his gloves back on.

Mr. PilgrimWay came close to the wall of clear ice. His face almost touched it. "I could take the Art from you," he said.

Tommy shook his head. "You would have taken it already if that were true."

Mr. PilgrimWay stepped back, smiled. "Very good," he said. "In my world, you might have risen to the Seats of the Reced." He looked behind Tommy at all the yellow flags. "It will not be long before this land is taken from you."

"Maybe," said Tommy.

"Certainly," said Mr. PilgrimWay. "It will be the loss of one of the things those you love hold most dear. It will be the loss of what your mother held most dear. But I could be at the Planning Commission meeting, Tommy Pepper. You know I can be persuasive. If you want your land, I will speak and give it to you. And afterward, I will only want the Art of the Valorim. And then I will depart with the O'Mondim sand, and you will never hear of us again. A fair agreement, especially since the Art of the Valorim was never meant to come to you."

Tommy looked up and down the beach. He looked back at the house, where Patty was reading by the fireplace, where his father had started to paint again.

And on the other side of the ice wall, Mr. PilgrimWay drew his own pictures. The story of Hengaelf and the Long Woods of Benu, gone for his folly. Of Wig and the Plains of Arnulf, and how he foolishly lost the Plains to the Arnalt. The tale of the raging of the Rignaulf and the destruction of the fruitlands of the Valley of the Denvelf, so that all that was left was wrack and ruin and havoc.

"One who would have risen to the Seats of the Reced would not be so foolish as Rignaulf," said Mr. PilgrimWay.

Tommy felt himself almost nod.

"Doesn't your land mean more to you than a world that lies beyond even the farthest stars you can see?" said Mr. PilgrimWay.

Tommy put his hand against the thrygeth wall.

"Or would you betray your mother again?" said Mr. PilgrimWay.

The night of the next Planning Commission meeting came, dark and metal cold. It was snowing again, lightly. Wisps of snow snaked along the road as the Peppers drove into town.

The meeting room was mostly full. Board members sat behind their long table up front. Mrs. Lumpkin and her lieutenant governor husband and her lawyers milled around and grinned and Mr. Lumpkin shook hands and grasped elbows. Neighbors from up and down the coast settled into the folding chairs, glad it was the Peppers' land up for easement and not their own.

And the Peppers sat close together, opposite Mrs. Lumpkin, who would not look at them. Patty wore her pink backpack with enough coloring books in it in case she got bored. Tommy fussed with his coat. It looked like it needed at least two new patches.

And Mr. PilgrimWay stood by the wall near the front row. He looked at Tommy and smiled and nodded, as if there was something between them.

The meeting room was hot after the outside cold.

Everything smelling wet. Everything in slow motion. More folding chairs being dragged up from the basement and squeaked open. Mrs. Lumpkin's husband still not sitting down. The meeting starting late. Agendas distributed. Finally the gavel to begin. Board attendance called, when everyone could already see who was there, for heaven's sake. Reading the minutes from the last meeting. Corrections. Approval of the revised minutes.

It looked to be a very long meeting.

Tommy wanted to take his folding chair and throw it across the room.

He looked at Mr. PilgrimWay, who was looking back through his shadowed eyes.

The Planning Commission now turning to Old Business. The bid for the sewage pipe repairs from Main Street down to Water Street. Discussion of costs. Discussion of timetables. Discussion of whether the town should solicit more bids. The question called. All those in favor of accepting the sewage bid, please say aye. All those opposed? The motion to accept the bid passes.

Tommy really wanted to take his folding chair and throw it across the room.

The question of an exemption for the zoning of the new development on the northeast side of Plymouth. Discussion of the zoning code. Discussion of the developer's proposal. Discussion of the additional traffic to that side of town. All those in favor? All those opposed? The nays have it. The variance is denied, pending further revisions to the development plan.

Tommy had to hold himself down in his folding chair.

Mr. PilgrimWay had not moved.

To New Business. Request for an easement along the north shore by Lumpkin and Associates Realtors.

Tommy stopped squirming—but he didn't stop wanting to throw his folding chair across the room. He felt Patty take his hand.

Mr. PilgrimWay turned to look back at him.

Mrs. Lumpkin asked to rise and present any additions to her PilgrimWay Condominium proposal to the Planning Commission.

Mrs. Lumpkin rising and presenting loudly and quickly.

Mr. PilgrimWay watching Tommy. Patty holding Tommy's hand.

Mrs. Lumpkin still talking. New jobs. New infrastructure. New economic boost for the town businesses. New tax base.

Her lawyers getting up to speak. They, too, speaking loudly and quickly.

Mr. PilgrimWay still watching Tommy.

The Planning Commission asking Mr. Pepper for anything he might have to say as a principal in the matter of this easement.

One of Mrs. Lumpkin's lawyers rising suddenly to remind the Planning Commission that Lumpkin and Associates Realtors reserve the right to sue the town and the Planning Commission if the easement is not granted, and to sue Mr. Pepper for slander if he speaks even one defamatory word against Lumpkin and Associates Realtors or Mrs. Lumpkin or any of her associates.

Mr. Pepper rising and opening his hands wide. It has been his family's land for generations, he says, and each generation has faithfully tended it. Should a rich Realtor now be free to take it simply because she wanted to take it? And as he had said last month, wasn't there need for some open space along the ocean coast that had not already been fenced off?

Tommy sees Mr. PilgrimWay shake his head. Not enough. Not nearly enough.

Mr. Pepper sits down.

All right, then. Are there any more speakers to this request for an easement? asks the Planning Commission.

Mr. PilgrimWay watching Tommy.

And Tommy wonders, *Does* he care more about a world beyond even the farthest stars he can see than about the land his mother loved?

A board member calls the question.

Should he give the Art of the Valorim to Mr. PilgrimWay?

"All those in favor of approving the easement on the Peppers' property, please say aye."

What would it mean to be betrayed into endless and eyeless Silence?

"All those opposed?"

What would his mother say to an O'Mondim without a face?

Tommy stood and looked at Mr. PilgrimWay. "No," he said loudly.

Mr. PilgrimWay did not move, but the shadows across his eyes changed. Darker.

"Young man, only members of the Planning Commission may vote. All those members of the Planning Commission opposed?"

Tommy looked at Mr. PilgrimWay.

"It's not too late," said Mr. PilgrimWay.

"She would never have given you the Art," he said, and turned away.

He knew the land was gone. He felt its loss like a hole punched out of the middle of his chest. How many things that he counted on being there forever would be gone someday?

"The motion on the easement on said property passes."

Gone. Just like that. Gone.

Tommy and Patty and their father walked down the aisle together.

Tommy did not look back at Mr. PilgrimWay.

The Long Woods of Benu once stretched farther than any other woods in the world. The trees were the tallest, the greenest, the thickest, and the sounds of their branches moving slowly in the winds, even the slightest winds, was mighty. The trees were as old as the mountains they stood beneath, and some believed that in their age, they had grown knowing and wise—and this Hengaelf felt when he walked beneath them, their leaves so thick that even the Twin Sunlight could not reach him, and the air sparkled, illil.

But Hengaelf had lost it in a bargain for an orlu—an orlu of ancient fashioning, but still, only an orlu.

And the trees had been hacked down.

The world would never see their like again.

That's what it felt like, thought Tommy.

Tommy and Patty pushed through the metal doors and so came out under the night sky. Their father came behind them and stood with his arms around them both.

Tommy smiled. The sky had cleared while they were inside, and now the stars brightened and pulsed in the cold, icy air. He squeezed Patty's hand.

The land was gone.

But he hadn't betrayed his mother. He *knew* he hadn't betrayed his mother.

At least there was that.

"Let's go home," said Mr. Pepper.

"I'm going to walk," said Tommy.

His father looked up at the sky. "It's pretty cold," he said.

"I'll be all right," said Tommy, and his father hugged him close, and Patty hugged him close, and they went to the car.

Tommy's father was right: it *was* cold. So cold that his feet squeaked the snow as he walked down toward the ocean and crossed onto Water Street. So cold that he didn't want to breathe in too deeply because the air would freeze his lungs.

Even the soft yellow lights on the Plymouth Rock pavilion looked cold tonight. Tommy put his gloved hands up in his armpits and his chin down into the collar of his coat. He wondered how many quarters were lying on Plymouth Rock. Or if it would be iced over.

He had not betrayed her. And he . . . felt okay.

More okay than he had felt for a long time.

Okay.

He smiled under the stars.

He figured Plymouth Rock would definitely be iced over with this kind of cold. Still smiling—he felt okay!—he walked into the pavilion and looked down.

The O'Mondim was standing on Plymouth Rock, his faceless head turned up toward Tommy.

Nothing on his face but his mouth—and the mark from Tommy's chain that had called him to life.

Water dripping from the seaweed that draped him.

He held his ruined right hand against his chest as if to protect it.

His other hand held his trunc.

And the O'Mondim's fah smell came over the pavilion wall, even in this cold.

Tommy backed away, then sprinted across Water Street. He turned around to see the O'Mondim leap over the pavilion fence.

Tommy ran up toward Burial Hill—and he didn't care if the cold froze his lungs. He passed the two churches and clambered up among the old gravestones, slipping back in the icy snow and scrambling up and slipping back and scrambling up from stone to stone to stone until he reached the top, breathless, his eyes watery—but still clear enough to see the O'Mondim starting up Burial Hill after him.

He moved easily through the deep snow, following the path Tommy had left.

Tommy felt the chain warm.

He took off his gloves and held up his hands. He spread his fingers, and then pushed against the cold air.

The snow on the hill beneath him gathered itself, and then it fell toward the O'Mondim—hard and icy and brittle, hurtling over and past the ancient gravestones and throwing the O'Mondim onto his back and covering him as it avalanched down.

Tommy watched. The snow piled between the two churches in jagged hunks.

Tommy breathed heavily. So cold in his lungs.

The snow stopped.

Then, one of the jagged hunks heaved up.

Tommy clambered through the snow to the far side of Burial Hill, and he began to slide down—which wasn't hard since it was mostly ice. But when he broke through, the snow was hip-deep, and he wallowed in it frantically, thrashing in it with his hands to get down to the lower wall—which he fell over. He smacked his knee onto the cold stones of the street—and it was, of course, his left knee, which was bruised anyway.

Above him, the O'Mondim had reached the top of Burial Hill.

Tommy ran as best he could with a left knee that was telling him to stop at every step. Down toward the ocean again, but he decided he didn't want to get too close to the water. He sprinted—sort of—down Court Street, crossed over to the Pilgrim Hall Museum, jumped onto its porch, and looked back from behind its stone pillars.

The O'Mondim was coming faster than something made out of sand should be able to come.

Tommy couldn't cross Main Street without being seen, so he ran behind the museum and down to Water

Street again. He was trembling—maybe because of the cold, maybe because he was sopping wet, maybe because he was being chased by a very large O'Mondim with a very large trunc. He passed the Plymouth Rock pavilion again and looked back.

The O'Mondim had his trunc raised high.

Tommy put his hand down to his left knee, and ran.

And ran.

And then, back across the street, he saw the lights on in the first grade hall of William Bradford Elementary School.

If the lights were on, maybe someone . . .

He crossed over to the school. He ran to the first grade side and pulled at the door. Locked.

He looked back. The O'Mondim saw him.

He ran around the building and over to the sixth grade door. The lights were on here, too, and he pulled at the door.

It opened.

Tommy ran inside.

"Hey, Mr. Zwerger," he hollered.

Nothing.

"Anyone! Hey, anyone!"

Nothing.

"Hey!"

He looked up and down the dead-end halls, still breathing heavily. Sweating. He didn't have any more time. He took off his coat and threw it down the hall toward his classroom.

Then he ran back outside. Across the parking lot. Behind the recycling bins. Waited, rubbing his left knee, trying not to breathe loudly.

The O'Mondim came around from the first grade side.

He pulled the sixth grade door out of its frame, broke it in two, and threw the pieces behind him.

He held his trunc with both hands—the way O'Mondim do—and went inside slowly. Tommy could see his faceless head turning toward each of the halls. Then, quickly, the O'Mondim raised the trunc higher, and started down the hall where his coat lay.

And the chain warmed, and Tommy . . . Tommy was filled with something he had never, ever expected: sadness.

Sadness for the O'Mondim. Sadness for his blindness. Sadness for his ruined hand. Sadness that he lived beneath a cold ocean.

That he was alone, the only one of his kind on the planet.

Sadness for the O'Mondim.

But he pushed the sadness down. He had to get home. And he was hurt. And it was getting colder—a lot colder— and his coat was lying in the sixth grade hallway. And he wasn't planning to go get it.

He crossed the parking lot and went back up to

Court Street. Then he headed north out of town, jogging to keep himself warm—until his knee hurt too badly, when he'd have to stop and rub it. Then he'd walk, and then jog until it hurt too much again. And that's how he made his way up along the coast, looking back over his shoulder for the O'Mondim, until he passed the sign for PilgrimWay Condominiums and climbed up the railroad-tie steps and so came to his house.

His house with no lights on.

No fire in the fireplace when he came in.

"Dad!" Tommy called. "Dad! Patty! I made it!

"Dad?"

It took him less than ten seconds to figure out that the dark house was deserted.

SEVENTEEN

The Journey of Ealgar, Who Would Be Called the Bold

So did Young Waeglim's heart laugh to hear the sounds of the Ethelim battering the gates of the Reced, and Ealgar laughed with him, running up the Tower stairs to the Forge of the Valorim. Their moods strengthened. What had seemed desperate chance now seemed hope.

But the Lord Mondus bent to the Tower door. In him the Silence welled up to terrible strength and the door splintered, even as the gates of the Reced heaved inward with the strength of arms of the Ethelim, who would no longer be stilled. The Ethelim burst into the Courts and then into the Great Hall, but with a shriek, the Lord Mondus, with Saphim the Cruel, did take to the steps of the Tower, the heat from the burning Forge lighting the way.

Young Waeglim heard them coming. "Do not be afraid," he spoke to Ealgar. "Now is the time for a strong heart and a strong mind. You will bring a new story to the Ethelim, a story that will be remembered even after the passing of the Valorim. If the Art of the Valorim is to be brought back to this world, it will be brought back by you."

Ealgar stood taller, though he was still a little fearful.

Young Waeglim put his hand on the shoulder of Ealgar. "Let the Art be brought back only for the good of this world. If it is in the hand of one who would use it for ill, in that world or this, then it will be upon you to destroy it—though its end means your own life-long exile."

"I will bring it back," said Ealgar. "I will put it into your hand."

Now the steps of the Lord Mondus and of Saphim the Cruel were close, and the only door that might hinder them had been shattered on the day that Brythelaf had been slain.

Young Waeglim spoke. "The days of the Valorim under the Twin Suns are over, and if a new world is to be made, then let it be by the Ethelim—by Ealgar the Bold, Ealgar of the Willing Heart. When you bring the Art of the Valorim back, wear it around your neck, upon your chest, and so will the Valorim be remembered, both for their terrible mistakes, and for their beauty."

Then did Young Waeglim kiss Ealgar on the fore-head, and Ealgar closed his eyes—and Young Waeglim, with the last of the Song left within him, in the heat of the Forge of the Valorim, did sing, and Ealgar was gone with the speed of Thought.

Young Waeglim watched from the top window of the Tower, and he saw the warm turning of the Twin Suns and felt their lovely light upon his skin. The sounds of the battle below fell from him, and he lifted his face to the sweet light. He drew his orlu, and turned.

Ealgar felt himself drawn softly from the Tower of the Reced, and when he opened his eyes, he was already looking down on his blue world, and passing by the first of the Twin Suns. He felt the heat of Hnaef, then that of Hengest. But hardly had he closed his eyes against their brightness than the Twin Suns were be-hind him, and the air cooled, and he looked, and saw the stars, so many stars, a greater host of stars than he imagined.

Ealgar reached up and touched the kiss of Young Waeglim upon his forehead, the kiss of the last of the Valorim. And then did his heart and his mind gladden, and he set his face toward the Art of the Valorim. He sped past the planets and stars whose ringing paths he had watched, and they fell behind him into the bright welter around his own now distant world. Then he saw stars and constellations he had never known, and so flew out of one galaxy, and ever more quickly, across long dark halls to the next, and then the next, speeding faster and faster and faster so that Ealgar could not count how many worlds and stars he passed.

Until, finally, he came to a small galaxy, and to a single small star at the edge of that galaxy, and to a small planet that rolled around it. He passed by its still moon and into its blue canopy, and he felt himself coming slower, and slower, and slower, and he passed through a mist of high white clouds and through their shadows and into the sunlight again, down through the air.

Slower, slower, and slower, until Ealgar felt himself stop, and he staggered upon the white shore of a blue sea—how strange to see it as blue as his own! He looked above him. A single sun that looked so lonely, trying to fill the whole sky with only its light. But the sound of the waves, and the feel of the sand beneath him, were as his own world—but cold.

And the kiss of the last of the Valorim was still on his forehead.

Ealgar wrapped his arms around himself for the chilled wind that blew from the water. Beside him, a field of tiny yellow pennants spread out, and beyond that, a small house.

Then he smelled the air—and the fah smell of the O'Mondim.

Ealgar took out the orlu of his father, and crouched. He looked up and down the beach, and then behind him, into the water. Nothing. But bitter was his mood, that the O'Mondim had found their fah way here before him. And bitter was the thought that already the Art of the Valorim might have been lost to him.

He stood and shivered again. What a cold world this was!

So Ealgar passed through the field of yellow pennants. He climbed up the broad steps of the sandy dune and to the door of the small house. He pushed it open. No sound from within. He walked inside. Then he saw the pale yellow wall and knew the work of the Art of the Valorim. He reached to touch it, but turned at a sound.

And looked into the faithless, shadowed eyes of Ouslim the Liar.

Ealgar raised his orlu.

EIGHTEEN

The O'Mondim

Tommy Pepper sat on the couch as one by one the policemen left, until Officer Goodspeed asked if he would like someone to stay outside and Tommy shook his head. "No."

"Is there someone I can call?" said Officer Goodspeed.

"No," said Tommy.

Officer Goodspeed said he'd be back in the morning. They'd find them. They'd already found the car by the Plymouth town offices. Officer Goodspeed was sure things would turn out all right.

Tommy said he'd be going up to bed now, and so Officer Goodspeed left.

Tommy was hungrier than he ever remembered being. He went into the kitchen and scrambled five eggs and brought them out on a plate and sat on the couch and watched the eggs until they got cold. Then he set the plate down on the floor.

Tommy went upstairs. He opened his window and leaned far out. He looked up and down the beach. Just in case.

Then he went to his bed, rolled his blankets tight around him, and cried until he was dark inside and out.

He cried for a long time, syn Githil aet Tinglaedu, nunc glaedre non, as if the sadness would never never never go away, but would stay, like Githil's sadness, inside him forever.

Tommy Pepper sat up suddenly. It was almost as if he could hear Githil's voice, crying out over the waves, as lonely as a single sun.

He rolled the blankets around him even more tightly.

It came again. Githil's cry.

He unrolled the blankets, ran to his window, and opened it. The moon was behind clouds and the ocean rough. Dark waves shattered on the shoreline, even up to the thrygeth wall. Nothing moving but the water, the high grasses, the yellow flags, and . . .

Tommy ran down the stairs and pushed open the front door. Immediately the fah stink of rotting seaweed covered him like ink, and he held his hand up to his mouth. He sprinted down the railroad-tie steps and through the yellow flags, and when he reached the shore, the moon dropped beneath the clouds, and through the ice wall, Tommy read these words in the sand:

PEPPER GIVE US WHAT WE WANT

Beside the words, half sunk into the sand, tied up with rotten seaweed, was Patty's pink backpack.

Tommy Pepper's eyes turned hard and narrowed.

Elder Waeglim standing at Brogum Sorg Cynna.

He looked out to sea and he took off his shirt. The cold wind blew against him, but he did not feel it at all. The green and silver of the chain shone brightly, shining onto the waves in front of him, and illuminating his chest so deeply that even his heart felt its keen light.

He ran around the ice wall, picked up Patty's backpack, and sprinted back up to the house.

He threw the backpack onto Patty's bed. She'd want it when she got home.

Then he went downstairs, the light of his chain still so bright. By the cellar doors he sorted through the garden tools until he found what he needed: the hoe and the shears. He laid them one on top of the other, and then he took off his chain and wrapped it around them.

"Ferr orlu," he whispered, and the chain grew brighter and brighter, until he could not see.

The first light of that cold morning saw policemen, phone calls, policemen, two reporters that the policemen hustled away, phone calls, policemen, more policemen at Tommy Pepper's house. Tommy sat on the couch, looking out the windows at the waving yellow flags between his home and the ocean. The house was stuffed with policemen—policemen who asked questions, who wanted pictures, who wondered if they had any enemies—and when was the last time you saw Patty? and how long has it been since she's talked? and have you seen anyone suspicious around the house? and has your father done anything like this before? and we'll need to take your sister's backpack to check for prints.

"No," said Tommy.

"It's routine," said the policemen.

"Find Mr. PilgrimWay," Tommy told them.

"Who?" they asked.

"Mr. PilgrimWay. Ask Mr. Zwerger."

They called William Bradford Elementary School from Tommy's kitchen. Did Mr. Zwerger know anything about a Mr. PilgrimWay?

"Who?" Mr. Zwerger told the policemen.

Tommy Pepper watched from his window as the policemen on the shore photographed the letters in the sand before the high tide came up to wipe them away.

As they finished, Officer Goodspeed drove up in his patrol car. He spoke to the policemen by the shore. They shook their heads and began to pack their equipment. Then Officer Goodspeed spoke to the policemen on the dune.

They shook their heads too, and headed to their patrol cars. Then Officer Goodspeed came up to the house, called for the policemen inside, spoke to them. And they headed down to their patrol cars—sort of angry.

Then Officer Goodspeed came inside.

"Listen," he said. "You've wasted a lot of people's time on a hoax."

"A hoax? My father and sister are missing."

"I spoke with Mr. PilgrimWay and he explained everything. You ought to be ashamed of yourselves, the whole lot of you."

"If you think—"

"He said he wouldn't press charges if you returned what belongs to him."

"And what's that?"

"You are in a heap of trouble, so let's not play games. Give me whatever it is that Mr. PilgrimWay wants and we'll call it even—and that's just because your father and I have been friends for so long. If it was anyone else . . ."

Tommy got up and looked out the windows. The policemen were almost all gone.

He went to the closet and slid out the wrapped canvas that Mrs. Lumpkin had brought back. He handed it to Officer Goodspeed. "Here," he said.

"Is this it?"

"This is it."

Officer Goodspeed took off the wrapping.

"He wanted a portrait of Mrs. Lumpkin?"

"Yup," said Tommy.

Officer Goodspeed returned the wrappings. He held his finger up at Tommy. "You keep your nose clean," he said. "I won't be as forgiving next time."

"I'll keep my nose clean," said Tommy.

When Officer Goodspeed got into his patrol car, Tommy reached under the couch and drew out his orlu. He balanced it lightly in his hand.

The policemen were all gone.

He was going to need some help.

He put the orlu back under the couch and headed to William Bradford Elementary School.

Tommy Pepper was not at his house when a brightness fell out of the sky and landed at the high-water mark by the shore.

On the morning after the Planning Commission meeting, Mr. PilgrimWay did not appear in Mr. Burroughs's classroom, and Tommy Pepper was late—not only because he missed the bus, but because he had to go back around to the first grade door since the sixth grade door had a sheet of plywood nailed across its empty frame.

Mrs. MacReady was sitting with the class, even though, she said, this was not what she was paid to do.

She suggested they all read quietly at their seats until a suitable substitute could be called in. They might choose any book they wished from the classroom library, and remember, reading is a Closed-Mouth Activity.

"Where is Mr. PilgrimWay?" said Alice Winslow.

"Where's Mr. Burroughs?" said Tommy.

"Did you not hear me say 'Closed-Mouth Activity'?" said Mrs. MacReady.

By ten o'clock, there was still no suitable substitute called in and Mr. Zwerger came to tell Mrs. MacReady she would have to stay with the class for a little longer.

Mrs. MacReady reminded them all that this was not what she was paid to do. So, she said, they should come up with a current event connected to the book they were reading and they should write a short essay that expressed how the book made them think differently about the current event and how this applied to their individual lives. They could take turns working at the computers, and those who were not working at the computers could compose rough drafts with pencil or pen. And writing, by the way, was also a Closed-Mouth Activity.

Alice Winslow held up her hand.

"What is it?" said Mrs. MacReady.

"Mr. Burroughs doesn't believe in Closed-Mouth Activities," she said.

Tommy looked at Alice Winslow and smiled. Maybe things could get back to normal.

Mrs. MacReady held the stack of white paper against herself. "Who?" she said.

"Our teacher, Mr. Burroughs," said Patrick Belknap.

Mrs. MacReady put the paper down on the desk.

"Who?" she said again.

"Mr. Burroughs," said James Sullivan. He shook his head and looked sort of surprised. "Mr. Burroughs is our teacher."

"Right," said Tommy.

"Mr. Burroughs," said Alice Winslow. She said it slowly, as it seeped back into her.

Tommy stood and walked over to the bulletin board. He ripped off the pictures of imagined planets, and with a black marker he quickly sketched the face of Mr. Burroughs. "Remember?" said Tommy. He pushed at the drawing with his left hand and the face turned the other way and began to smile. "Remember?" he said.

"Where is Mr. Burroughs?" said Patrick Belknap.

Mrs. MacReady came over to the board and looked at it closely. "You drew on the classroom bulletin board," said Mrs. MacReady. She took her glasses off and wiped at her eyes. "That looks like Mr. Burroughs," she said. She put her glasses back on. "Is that permanent marker?"

By noon, Mrs. MacReady let it be known that she had her own work to do on top of being a substitute teacher and as far as she knew, no one was doing it for her. So she would have to go back and forth between the main office and this classroom for a couple of hours, and she expected perfect behavior when she had to step out. If you were finished with your book, you could continue your essay on the relevant current event. If not, you should keep reading attentively. Both of these were still Closed-Mouth Activities. She would be back in a few minutes.

As soon as Mrs. MacReady left and her footsteps were sounding from far enough away, James Sullivan put down his book and turned to Tommy. "What happened to Mr. Burroughs?"

"I'm glad you remember Mr. Burroughs," said Tommy.

"How could I not remember Mr. Burroughs?"

"Good question. And he's not the only one missing."

He told them. He tried not to bawl like a first-grader.

"So Mr. Burroughs was the first one gone," said Alice Winslow. "Maybe if we found out where Mr. Burroughs went, that might be a clue to where Patty is."

"Thank you, Detective Winslow," said Patrick Belknap. "Do you want me to get out the bloodhounds now or after school?"

"You know, Patrick, you can sometimes be—"

"A maeglia, I know," said Tommy. "Listen, I think what we need to do is to arm ourselves."

This took a moment to understand.

"Arm ourselves?" said Alice Winslow.

"Arm ourselves!" said James Sullivan.

Tommy nodded. "Arm ourselves," he said again.

"Oh my goodness," said Alice Winslow.

And suddenly it seemed as if everything in the room grew hushed, and serious, and important.

"How?" said Patrick Belknap.

Tommy stood up. "We have to go," he said.

"MacReady will kill us if we're not here when she gets back," said Alice Winslow.

Tommy considered this for a moment. Then he looked at Cheryl Lynn Lumpkin. He walked over to her desk. "Cheryl Lynn," he said.

Cheryl Lynn looked up from her book.

"We have to go. Can you cover for us?"

"What?" said Cheryl Lynn.

"We need you to cover for us. Say we've gone to the bathroom."

"I'm not going to cover for you, jerk," said Cheryl Lynn.

"Not just me. Alice and Sullivan and Belknap, too."

"Really. All four of you. All gone to the bathroom. You expect me to tell MacReady that?"

"Not just that," said Tommy.

Tommy looked around, then he went to Patrick Belknap's desk and picked up the accordion that Patrick was keeping by his feet.

"Hey," said Patrick Belknap.

Tommy lugged the accordion to Cheryl Lynn Lumpkin's desk. Then he reached beneath his shirt and pulled out his chain. He grabbed Cheryl Lynn's hand— "What do you think you're . . . ?"—and he pressed the chain into her palm.

For a moment, it glowed sharply, then Tommy put it back under his shirt.

Cheryl Lynn looked down at the accordion case.

Patrick Belknap stood up.

"Belknap, it's all right," said Tommy.

Cheryl Lynn Lumpkin opened the accordion case. She grappled with the thing, and finally swung it out.

"I think I'd play something that sounded sort of Scottish," said Tommy.

Cheryl Lynn began to squeeze.

"Time to go," said Tommy, and—Patrick Belknap looking back—the four of them ran out of the classroom, and down the hall, and across to the first grade hall, and so outside.

Mrs. MacReady later said it was a song from her childhood. She couldn't believe Cheryl Lynn Lumpkin was playing it. Neither could Cheryl Lynn.

It wasn't long before Mrs. MacReady started to cry happily.

She never even knew they were gone.

* * *

Most days, it took Tommy about thirty-two minutes to walk from William Bradford Elementary School to his house. At a run, pausing for breath, he could do it in twenty-four, or maybe twenty-three if he was headed from his house to William Bradford, since it's mostly downhill that way.

They took about twenty-two. Who knew Alice Winslow could run so well?

Along the way, Tommy told them what they needed. He'd already made the orlu. Maybe another orlu for Sullivan. A halin for Alice. And a limnae for Belknap.

"How come I don't get an orlu?" said Patrick Belknap. "And what is an orlu?"

Tommy said he didn't know what exactly they were going to do, but somehow, somehow, he knew they'd have to wait for Mr. PilgrimWay to show up. And they'd be ready. "And whatever you do," he said, "eteth threafta."

They nodded.

"Sure," said Sullivan.

And as it turned out, Tommy was right about the first thing: they didn't know what exactly they were going to do. But he was wrong about the second thing.

They didn't have to wait.

It was a familiar sound—or one that felt familiar: the sound of two orluo, clashing.

Tommy ran behind the house, and there, in the pine

woods, he saw them: Mr. PilgrimWay and a shirtless boy who looked as if he might be his own age. Maybe just a little older, but almost the same height, and weight, and— well, almost everything. And the orluo were flashing between them, faster than Tommy could have imagined, and Tommy couldn't help but, with a pang, feel amazed and even a little jealous at how skilled the boy was.

"Tommy," yelled Alice Winslow, "we should call the police."

But Tommy ran into his house, and when he came out, he was shirtless too, and he carried his orlu.

"Tommy?" said Alice Winslow.

And suddenly, Mr. PilgrimWay was pressing the boy back down the dune, and the blows of his orlu were stronger and more powerful than those of the boy, who gave way, and gave way, back and back, falling once in the sand, and saved only when Tommy cried out and Mr. PilgrimWay looked up and Tommy swung at him with his orlu and Mr. PilgrimWay had to parry it and the boy scrambled away.

Mr. PilgrimWay smiled.

"Gumena weardas!" the boy yelled, and he pointed to the ground beyond the house—where the flags were blowing their little selves straight in with the sea breeze, and where the blocks of the thrygeth wall lay scattered.

Together, Tommy and the boy ran to the flags, with Mr. PilgrimWay only a few steps behind them, and there, they turned and stood beside each other, shoulder to shoulder.

The boy looked at James Sullivan and Patrick Belknap. He pulled his gyldn from his belt and threw it to them.

"I think he meant you to take it," said Patrick Belknap.

"It's closer to you," said James Sullivan.

"I'm not taking my shirt off. It's freezing."

"Oh my goodness," said Alice Winslow.

Mr. PilgrimWay ignored them, and smiled again at Tommy Pepper and the boy.

"Two boys against one who sits in the Seats of the Reced?" he said. "And only one of them Ethelim?"

Tommy figured that this was where they were supposed to say something noble and heroic, but the boy, who was holding his orlu out in front of him, said nothing. Tommy decided to shut up. But he held his orlu out in front of him too.

He wasn't exactly sure if he was holding it correctly—or if it was upside down.

Mr. PilgrimWay took a step closer.

And then he was upon them.

Tommy was sure that he was holding the orlu upside down.

If it had not been for the boy, Tommy Pepper would have been overwhelmed immediately; the rush forward was that quick. He tried to be a part of the battle, but really, the most he could do was to circle behind Mr. PilgrimWay and pretend he was a threat—at least he could keep Mr. PilgrimWay a little bit distracted. And maybe it worked, because even though the clash of his orlu did not come as loudly as the boy's, Mr. PilgrimWay did have to keep turning his head to see where Tommy was, and those were the moments—brief though they were—when the boy could let down his orlu and breathe.

"You know, Sullivan," Tommy called out, "I could use a little help."

"How do you hold this thing?" said James Sullivan.

"It's a gyldn," hollered Tommy.

"Oh, thanks," said Patrick Belknap. "That tells us a whole lot."

And then the three orluo clashed together and, in sparks and shrieks, locked, and Mr. PilgrimWay struck the boy in the face with his open hand, and the boy fell back to the sand, dazed. And Mr. PilgrimWay turned to Tommy.

He drew his own gyldn from behind him.

"See! That's how you hold it," said Alice Winslow.

Mr. PilgrimWay smiled again.

"Your orlu is upside down," he said.

Tommy turned it in his hands.

"Give me the chain."

Tommy looked behind Mr. PilgrimWay. The boy was shaking his head, trying to stand up, but still dazed.

"He will be no help to you. Give me the chain."

"Where's Patty?" said Tommy. "Where's my father?"

Mr. PilgrimWay took a step closer. He shook his head. "The chain first."

So did Tommim Pepper draw out again the Art of the Valorim, and show Ouslim the Liar the chain of the Art of the Valorim. And the boy Ealgar looked, and cried against the faithless Ouslim, who would take the Art of the Valorim and subdue his world.

And Tommim Pepper spoke. "No."

So did Ouslim the Liar come upon him again, and though his companions did rush to him—even unto Ealgar—they were thrown down, and Ouslim the Liar stood above him, and terrible was the speed of his orlu.

Then, in the battle's greatest need, did Tommim Pepper fight as did Elder Waeglim himself at Brogum Sorg Cynna, who, disdaining all armor and weaponry, did go out against his enemies with a gyldn, and only a gyldn, and his hands flew before his enemies like flighted birds, and none could pierce him, or wound him, so quickly and easily did the gyldn fly in front of him, and it seemed there were many more than one.

And Tommim Pepper laughed in his heart and swung his orlu, and glad was his mind when Ouslim stepped back before him, and back again, and back, until finally his feet were in the sea.

And Ouslim the Liar cried out to the O'Mondim, and again.

And the O'Mondim came.

And the O'Mondim went to Tommim Pepper and he took the orlu from his hand and threw it far under the waves, where none will see it again. Then he gripped the shoulder locks of Tommim Pepper and did drive him to the ground, and Ouslim the Liar held his bright orlu above his face and did say that there were none to save him now. And who was he, to challenge one who sat in the Seats of the Reced?

And it seemed to Tommim Pepper that he looked upon the setting sun for the last time in his days.

"Byrgum barut," said Tommim Pepper. "Su byrgum barut!"

Mr. PilgrimWay smiled. He pulled his orlu away and rested it on the sand. He looked around at Alice, and Belknap and Sullivan, at the young Ethelim, and then again at Tommy.

"This is pointless," he said. "You will give me the chain. You must give it to me, for the sleep that closes the eyes of your sister and your father will be only sleep for another day. Then it will be sleep no more. It will be death."

"I don't believe anything you say."

"Then you will live with the consequences of your unbelief." He looked over his shoulder. The sun had set not long ago and the darkness was coming quickly. "It isn't a long time, and when I come back, you will give me the chain of your own will." He pointed to the boy. "Remember, he will want the chain for his own purposes—but those are not your purposes."

Tommy shook his head. "Liar," he said.

Mr. PilgrimWay smiled. "A sign, then, of good faith." He looked at the O'Mondim, and suddenly his orlu whirled and hit the O'Mondim across the chest, who fell on the sand and lay still. Mr. PilgrimWay turned back to Tommy. "The Art of the Valorim gave him life. So it can take it away." He pointed. "There is the mark you drew across his face. Use the chain now to erase it and this clod will dissolve into the grains from which he was made. That is my act of good faith." He stepped back.

Tommy got up, slowly. He watched Mr. PilgrimWay, and watched the O'Mondim, who did not move as he came closer. Who did not move as he gripped his chain. Who did not move as Tommy looked at the mark he could erase—already harder to see in the darkening light.

The O'Mondim.

"Ferr," said the boy.

But Tommy Pepper whispered, "What is your name?"

"The O'Mondim have no names," said Mr. PilgrimWay.

Tommy looked at Mr. PilgrimWay. "They used to," he said. He looked back at the O'Mondim. "What is your name?"

"Tommy Pepper," said Mr. PilgrimWay, "you speak to sand."

But Tommy knew this was a terrible lie.

Tommy stepped back from the O'Mondim. He took his hand from the chain and shook his head again. "I won't," he said. He looked at Mr. PilgrimWay. "We're *not* the same."

Mr. PilgrimWay laughed, suddenly, harshly. He motioned to the O'Mondim, who stood up, slowly, awkwardly without his right hand.

"A day, Tommy Pepper. And then you will give me the chain."

Another motion to the O'Mondim, who turned and walked toward the sea. Tommy watched him pass through the blocks of clear thrygeth ice and into the waves. And in that light he could not be sure, but before the O'Mondim sank beneath the water, it seemed that he turned back to Tommy for a moment—only a moment—and then he was gone.

And Mr. PilgrimWay walked away along the beach down toward Plymouth, and was covered in the gathering darkness.

"I still don't think I'm holding this right," said James Sullivan.

Tommy looked at him. "It doesn't look like it."

The O'Mondim had turned his sightless face back toward him.

They helped the boy up to the house, and Tommy got one of his sweatshirts for him. It fit pretty well. Then he went into the kitchen and he and Sullivan made peanut butter sandwiches—which turned out to be something the boy had never seen before, but he was hungry enough that it didn't matter—while Belknap worked at building a fire, and the living room filled first with smoke and then with the wood's dry heat. The boy could not understand anything that Alice Winslow or James Sullivan or Patrick Belknap said, and they couldn't understand anything he said, but Tommy translated as he brought peanut butter sandwiches and kindling back and forth down the yellow hall, his mother's image walking beside him each time.

And when Tommy finally sat down, Patrick Belknap pointed at the boy and said, "Who is he?"

The boy touched his face and said, "Ealgar." He waited, then said, "Ealgar Ethelim."

There was a long pause.

"He's not from our world," said Tommy Pepper.

Another very long pause.

"No kidding," said James Sullivan.

And Alice Winslow said, "Tell us everything."

So Tommy did. And when he finished, Alice and Sullivan and Belknap called home to let their folks know they were sleeping over at the Peppers' house that night—it being a Friday—and the five, with one orlu and one gyldn, prepared to guard themselves through the dark hours.

Tommy and Alice made some more peanut butter sandwiches. Then they found enough sleeping bags and blankets and pillows while Ealgar tried to teach Sullivan and Belknap how to handle a gyldn. He was shivering, so they stayed close to the fire. "Dur, weard," said Ealgar, his arms clasped around himself. Tommy brought him his woolen blanket, and he wrapped it around his shoulders. Then Tommy brought more wood inside and they built up the fire to a roar.

The night was dead dark, so they all decided to stay awake to keep the fire lit and to watch. But a battle with one of the faithless Valorim will take its toll, and one by one they fell into deep sleep. None of them made it to midnight.

Except Tommy Pepper.

Tommy pushed back his blankets and got up. He looked around: they were all still asleep. He threw two logs on the fire, then went to the windows and looked out at the dark night, the dark sea, the dark clouds so thick that he could barely see where the moon was shining behind them. No stars at all.

Patty. His father.

His mother.

He looked back at the boy from another world. If he gave Mr. PilgrimWay the chain . . .

But Patty. His father.

Tommy took the chain off. He twisted it around his hand.

He had had enough.

He had had enough.

"I'm sorry," he whispered to Ealgar.

Patty. His father.

Holding the chain in his fist, he pressed it against his heart. Then, carefully, he opened the front door, and carefully he closed it behind him. Tommy sat down on the stoop and waited in the cold dark, holding out the chain in the palm of his hand.

He sang the song of Githil—though he hardly knew he was singing it. Or maybe it was the Bach.

Whichever one it was, it did not take long.

Tommy did not see the O'Mondim walk out of the water, but he knew he was on the beach. When the waves burst to whiteness behind him, Tommy saw the O'Mondim's outline, a slash against the white.

Tommy walked down to the shore, through the field of yellow flags. He may have been crying. He was near enough now that even in the dark, he could see the O'Mondim clearly. And Tommy held out his hand, where the Art of the Valorim rested in his palm, the chain dur.

He waited for the O'Mondim to come take it.

But he didn't.

Tommy waited.

The O'Mondim did not move.

The O'Mondim did not move.

Tommy could smell the fah smell of the O'Mondim in the air.

"Here it is," he said. "You wanted it, so here it is." He held his hand out even farther.

The O'Mondim did not move.

"Here it is," Tommy screamed. And he closed his hand on the Art of the Valorim, the chain that had traveled through unimaginable reaches of space, faster than light itself, and he threw it across the yellow flags, and it landed in the dark sand at the feet of the O'Mondim.

The O'Mondim did not move.

"Take it!" screamed Tommy. "Take it! Take it!"

Slowly, slowly the O'Mondim bent down to the sand, his long left arm reaching. Slowly, slowly he scooped it from the sand. Slowly, slowly he straightened himself.

And then, and then, he held the chain out to Tommy Pepper, and he raised his other, ruined hand, and he held that out too.

The sea quieted. The wind dropped. The moon

opened the clouds and shone a single silver beam upon the two of them, Tommy Pepper and the O'Mondim, Tommy with his arms folded around himself, shivering in the dark, and the O'Mondim with his arms out, holding the Art of the Valorim.

Tommy heard the door to his house open behind him, and he knew that the boy—Ealgar Ethelim—had come out.

And he didn't want Ealgar to see, but he couldn't help it: Tommy really was crying.

The O'Mondim stepped into the field of yellow flags, his long legs shuffling across the beach. The moon came out more as he came closer, both arms still before him, the chain shining brightly in the O'Mondim's palm, Tommy still crying, and crying, and crying, and the smell of the seaweed strong around them, until the O'Mondim stood close, almost touching Tommy.

And he held out the chain to him.

"What do you want me to do?" said Tommy.

The O'Mondim held out his ruined hand.

"I never meant . . ."

Tommy felt Ealgar beside him. "He knows you," he whispered.

The O'Mondim's ruined hand touched Tommy's chest.

So cold, so cold, so cold.

So lonely.

"You are Valorim," said Ealgar, and he bowed his head.

Tommy reached out to the O'Mondim and took the chain. He put it back around his neck. Immediately the chain was hot on his chest.

And as if he were in a dream, Tommy Pepper took the good hand of the O'Mondim, and looked up to his sightless face, and said, "We need to go where the sand is wetter."

Hand in hand, Ealgar following, Tommy Pepper and the O'Mondim walked back through the yellow flags to the sand where the tide was rising. There the O'Mondim lay down and stretched out his ruined arm. And Tommy formed the wet sand into a hand around the ruin, shaping the fingers and the wrist, and bringing sand to flesh until it was connected, all the while the tide rising and the O'Mondim lying as still as lifeless stone.

And when he was finished with the hand, Tommy—quickly because the water was breaking so near—Tommy took sand in his own hand, and reached to the O'Mondim's face. And with the sand, he formed two eyes, and a nose, and two ears, all below the line he had formed on the O'Mondim's forehead with the Art of the Valorim.

And still the O'Mondim lay without moving.

Tommy stepped back when the first wave reached them. It came up against the O'Mondim's body and Tommy could only imagine the chill of the dark water. The next wave was a little less, but then the next came in higher and splashed against the O'Mondim, who lay on the sand, still unmoving.

Tommy backed away as more and more waves came up against the O'Mondim, and then over the O'Mondim, until the water from the spent wave rushing back over the O'Mondim was not gone before the next wave came upon him. And so the tide came in, and though the moon now threw aside the clouds and shone fully down upon the beach, Tommy could no longer see the O'Mondim in the waves.

Gone.

Tommy and Ealgar walked back up to the house, opened the front door, closed it against the cold, and fell at the bottom of the stairs, dead asleep.

NINETEEN

The Last Battle of Young Waeglim

For many, many winters will the battle between Young Waeglim the Noble and the Lord Mondus be remembered. Long may it be told to honor the last of the Valorim of that world.

When the door to the Forge of the Valorim was breached, and when the Lord Mondus and Saphim were upon him, orluo drawn, then did Young Waeglim the Noble laugh, glad-hearted, at their confusion. "So has the boy gone out of this world," said Young Waeglim, "and so none may follow." And with a blow of his orlu, he struck the Forge of the Valorim, and the white heat of it filled the Tower Room, and he struck it again, and the Forge of the Valorim fell to ruin around his feet.

Then did Saphim the Cruel cry out against Young Waeglim, and rush upon him, and thrust his orlu through the shoulder of Young Waeglim. But short was *his triumph. Young Waeglim drew the orlu of Saphim from his shoulder and turned it upon the Councilman, so that Saphim the Cruel fell among the ruins of the Forge of the Valorim, and moved no more.*

Then did the Lord Mondus, the last of the rulers of the O'Mondim save Ouslim the Liar, who had left that world, cry out upon Young Waeglim, and move against him, attacking the wounded shoulder of the warrior. Grim was the face of the Lord Mondus, and his orlu flashed down again and again. But bold was the face of Young Waeglim, and though sore wounded and hard-pressed, and with little hope, he fought on against the attack of the Lord Mondus.

Great was the battle they fought in the Tower Room of the Reced through that morning, to past noon, through the late day, and so toward First Sunset. Grievous the wounds, and hard. But neither would yield or give ground. And as the ruined Forge at their feet cooled and the room grew darker, so did Young Waeglim hear the brave cries of the Ethelim, and he knew that though the O'Mondim were great and many, they would fall that day.

Blithe was Young Waeglim's heart, though mortal his many wounds.

Then did the Lord Mondus strike down against Young Waeglim's bloodied shoulder, so that he cried out against the hurt, and stepped back to the very edge of the Tower window. All who fought below turned to him—even the sightless faces of the O'Mondim, who knew that the last of the Valorim was above them, and who held their weapons still.

And all began to grow dark and darker for Young Waeglim. And the Lord Mondus did strike him again upon the shoulder wound that Saphim the Cruel had given, and Young Waeglim did fall upon the outermost ledge, and stillness gripped those beneath the Tower.

The last light of Hnaef blew out.

And Young Waeglim did of a sudden reach behind the knee of the Lord Mondus, and pull, and so together, as the Lord Mondus shrieked, the two fell from the Tower Room.

Those below watched their terrible fall, wailing at the end of Young Waeglim—even those among the O'Mondim host, who had once held the Valorim as their good lords.

But then, from out of this world, a green shining light flew downward—faster than Thought itself. It spun beside the Tower of the Reced, faster than eye could see, and gripped the falling Young Waeglim and held him aloft. The Ethelim shielded their eyes against its brightness, and the green light carried Young Waeglim up. And Young Waeglim—who had thought his spirit would leave him—was brought back into the

Tower Room, among the ruins of the Forge, and set down so gently that he could not tell when he had left the air.

But for the Lord Mondus, there was none to save him.

TWENTY

What Was Lost and What Was Found

In the morning, Tommy woke to the sound of Ethelim curses.

He looked around.

Ealgar was gone.

He ran into the living room and hollered, "Gumena weardas! Sullivan! Belknap! Alice! Gumena . . . Oh, forget it." He grabbed the gyldn, ran outside, and sprinted down the dune.

But it wasn't Mr. PilgrimWay. Or the O'Mondim.

It was Mrs. Lumpkin and her yellow Mazda.

"What in the world is going on here?" Mrs. Lumpkin yelled. She got out of her car and walked among the trampled and scattered yellow flags. She looked at Tommy. "Again? You pulled the flags out again?"

She was not, Tommy figured, happy.

She began to climb the dune, and Tommy would later admit that she did seem to be sort of threatening. "If you think for one moment that I'm going to let things slide again . . ." began Mrs. Lumpkin.

"Vitrie!" cried Ealgar.

She turned back to him. "What did you just call me?"

Ealgar drew his orlu and began waving it across the yellow Mazda.

She turned back to Tommy. "What did he just call me?"

Ealgar said something that Tommy thought he probably shouldn't translate.

"I'm not sure," he said.

She began walking back down the dune toward Ealgar—which was pretty brave of her. "Do you know how expensive it is to fix a scratch on a Mazda?" she said. "If you touch that car, you'd better have some good insurance!"

Ealgar's orlu touched the car. All along its driver's side. And across the hood. And then down through the front grille, and then deep into the radiator, which began to leak into the sand.

Mrs. Lumpkin gave a startled gasp.

The orlu went through the windshield.

Mrs. Lumpkin gave a startled screech.

She sort of ran the last few steps to her car, opened the door, turned the key in the ignition.

She didn't have to close the door, because Ealgar's orlu took it off for her.

She put the car into gear and pressed the accelerator. For a moment the wheels spun in the sand, but then they caught and the car reversed through the field of yellow flags, and Mrs. Lumpkin yelled something of her own that Tommy figured he shouldn't translate either—and then she whipped past Ealgar, but not before his orlu had sheared off the left fender.

"I wasn't kidding about the insurance," hollered Mrs. Lumpkin, and she gunned the yellow Mazda toward town.

Tommy wasn't sure if the Mazda would make it or not.

Ealgar put up his orlu, climbed the dune, nodded at Tommy, and went into the house.

"All right, then," Tommy said, and followed.

They ate peanut butter sandwiches for breakfast. Even Ealgar. They split what was left of the orange juice. Ealgar wouldn't touch it. He wrapped his arms around himself, and it *was* dur outside, so Tommy kept the fire roaring and Ealgar didn't go far from it.

When he wasn't keeping the fire roaring, Tommy paced.

And paced.

Elder Waeglim at Brogum Sorg Cynna.

He had to do something.

"You are driving me crazy," said James Sullivan.

"Look—it's not your sister or your father out there somewhere and who knows what's happening to them."

"So we go find them. Where do we start?"

"Dang, Sullivan, why didn't I think of that? Why don't I try to figure out where we should look? That seems like it might be a good idea."

"Selith, Tommim, selith," said Ealgar.

"All right, I'm sorry. But I haven't slept much and when I do sleep I dream about being chased by an O'Mondim and when I wake up there's a battle with Mrs. Lumpkin's car and I have four"—he felt his sides— "no, five cuts from Ouslim's orlu and they sting like all get-out and I still don't know where my father and sister are."

"You weren't chased by the O'Mondim, Pepper. He came out of the water and lay down."

"Actually, Belknap, since you weren't there that night, you don't know that I *was* chased by the O'Mondim, starting with Plymouth Rock until I lost him at school."

"You ran to the school?"

"The lights were on."

James Sullivan called from the kitchen. "You know, I found seven eggs here. And I think some bacon, but it looks kind of old. Do you mind if I—"

"Why were the lights on?" said Alice.

* * *

It was snowing by the time they passed Plymouth Rock and headed up to William Bradford Elementary School. Ealgar was wearing two sweatshirts and Mr. Pepper's pea coat, and even though his face was set hard, he looked around at the falling flakes and, Tommy saw, even tried catching them on his tongue. He held his orlu, and Tommy, running in front of them all, held the gyldn. He was limping a little bit.

They ran to the sixth grade side.

"You know," said Alice—and it took her a while to say this, since she was breathing pretty heavily—"we could get in real trouble for breaking into school."

Ealgar leaned forward and put his hand on the plywood across the sixth grade door. Then he turned to Tommy and pointed at Alice Winslow, then James Sullivan, then Patrick Belknap. "Gumena weardas?" he said.

Tommy shook his head.

"Nanig?"

"Nope."

Ealgar stared at the plywood again.

"What did he say?" said James Sullivan.

"He asked if any of you were warriors."

"And you said no?"

Tommy looked at him. "What should I have said?"

"Yes, you jerk," said James Sullivan.

The wind came up against them from the ocean, and

they all saw that it was not . . . right. The snow swirled at their faces, no matter which way they looked, and it stung.

Ealgar turned. One by one he looked at them, and then he turned to Tommy. "Gumena weardas," he said. He turned to Alice Winslow. "Gumena weardas," he said again. And again to James Sullivan. And again to Patrick Belknap. "Gumena weardas."

And they all stood a little firmer against the wind, and felt something strong and deep within them stirring.

Ealgar turned again to the plywood across the door.

The wind colder and pushing hard against them, almost shoving them back. The gray sky letting go more flakes. A dark squall gathering over the ocean, moving toward them quickly.

"Nu schulon habbe heardre earmas, heale cenre, mod bealda," said Ealgar.

"He really is from another world," said Patrick Belknap.

"We could still get in a whole lot of trouble if . . ."

Two slashes of the orlu and the plywood lay in splinters.

". . . we break in," said Alice Winslow.

Ealgar and Tommy stepped into the halls of William Bradford Elementary School, and then Alice Winslow, and James Sullivan, and Patrick Belknap too—who got inside just before the dark squall hit them. But it brought, with the snow, the rucca smell of decaying seaweed.

The halls were empty and dark, with that strange feeling that school halls have when they're not filled with kids getting to class. No one hollering, no bells, no slamming lockers, no crumpled-up papers being kicked along, no teacher directing traffic, no smells from the school cafeteria or the gym or the science room. Every step they took echoed. They didn't want to talk. They didn't want to breathe.

"I'm going to go get my accordion," said Patrick Belknap.

"What?" said James Sullivan.

"My accordion. I left it—"

"You know what, Belknap? Warriors do not carry accordions. They never carry accordions. They don't even like accordions."

"This one does."

"Which only goes to show that—"

"Shut up," said Tommy.

James Sullivan and Patrick Belknap figured that's what Ealgar told them too.

They followed the sixth grade hall and looked through the windows into the classrooms. Everything was dark. All the desks were in janitorial order. No one, anywhere.

They turned around and went back toward the other halls.

No one in the fourth or fifth grade hallways.

They turned around and came back.

No one in the cafeteria.

No one in the gym. No one in the locker rooms—and Alice Winslow checked the girls' locker room by herself, which Tommy said goes to show who the real gumena weardas was.

No one in the auditorium. They even checked on stage behind the curtain, and in the band room, and in the instrument storage room, and in Mrs. Low's piano practice room.

No one.

They went to the second and third grade halls.

No one.

And then all the way down the first grade hall.

No one.

Until they turned around.

And Tommy saw the O'Mondim standing, almost touching the ceiling, his two good hands dangling low by his knees.

His eyes were watching them.

"Fah," said Ealgar, and he raised his orlu over his shoulder.

But Tommy held Ealgar's arm, and by himself, he walked down the dark first grade hallway. The O'Mondim was so still, so unmoving.

Except he was singing—humming really.

The Bach piece.

Tommy's breath left him. And he heard her as clearly as if she were standing beside him: "Oh, Tommy, I love to hear you play. Especially the Bach. I want to cry when I hear you play the Bach. I want to cry because it's so beautiful."

Tommy looked at the face of the O'Mondim.

Something had scratched out most of the line the Art of the Valorim had made on the O'Mondim's forehead, and now he was turning back to the sand he was made of. He seemed to be crumbling around the edges. His new eyes were almost gone.

"Fah," said Ealgar again.

Tommy shook his head, and he took the chain from under his shirt and held it toward the O'Mondim's face.

But the O'Mondim did not bend his face down to him. Instead, with his right hand, he pointed to the school basement door.

Then Ealgar was beside him. He looked down at Tommy's hand.

"Ars Valorim," he said, and shook his head. "Ne cynna se weoruld. Na se weoruld." He held out his hand.

"Not yet," said Tommy Pepper.

"Nefer se weoruld," he said.

"After we've found Patty," he said.

"Are we going down there or not?" said James Sullivan.

"We're going down there," said Alice Winslow.

She walked over and tried the doorknob.

"It's probably . . ." began Patrick Belknap.

Alice Winslow looked around, then took the gyldn from Tommy's hand and smashed it through the wire window in the door.

". . . locked."

Alice Winslow reached through the glass and opened the door. Then she gave the gyldn back to Tommy.

"Gumena weardas," said Ealgar.

Tommy flipped on the switch and a small light came on at the bottom.

And Tommy went down, then Ealgar, then Alice Winslow and James Sullivan and Patrick Belknap. Down the stairs without speaking, the dry metal scent of basement all around them.

At the bottom, it was as dur as it was outside.

And as still.

Ealgar held up his orlu.

Tommy took the last four steps at a jump. He couldn't help it. He didn't care if anyone heard. He grabbed the handle of the metal door at the bottom of the stairs and pulled on it.

Locked.

It took five swipes with the orlu to tear it open, and Tommy leaped through the shredded metal.

"Dad! Patty! Patty!"

He flipped on the light switch.

"It's me!"

And stretched out on the cement floor, close to the school furnaces, was Mr. Burroughs—very pale and very still.

And beyond Mr. Burroughs, Tommy saw his father.

And next to him Patty—Patty!—who was up on one arm as if she were just waking but still couldn't move, and whose eyes were impossibly wide open.

Eyes looking behind him.

He took a step toward her, and he felt sleep pouring over him like the ocean, wave after wave, so heavy, so heavy, that all he could think about was lying down and closing his eyes. It was all he could think about. So heavy. He could hardly hear the cries on the steps above him, and even those sounds began to seem as if they came from farther and farther away, so far away that they had nothing at all to do with him.

He took another step toward Patty, and it was so hard to move his legs, since they seemed weighted with Patty's white stones. For a moment he thought of touching the chain, but the idea of bringing his hand up was ridiculous. Impossible. Everything was so heavy.

Tommy Pepper closed his eyes.

And then, Tommy heard the Bach piece. From high above him, the Bach piece.

It was so beautiful, it made him want to cry.

And someone slapped his face. Hard.

He opened his eyes.

"Patty," he said.

She pointed.

Tommy turned, and through the shattered metal door, he saw Ealgar with his orlu swinging high above his head. And Alice Winslow, James Sullivan, and Patrick Belknap behind him, all hollering.

And Mr. PilgrimWay.

Tommy shook himself, and again. "Patty," he said.

Ealgar was hacking at Mr. PilgrimWay's orlu, hacking and hacking with everything in him. And step by step, Mr. PilgrimWay was forced back and back up the cellar steps that led outside.

Tommy shook himself, still trying to get the sleep out of his head.

"Tommim!" called Ealgar.

Tommy ran out—sort of—onto the stairs, ducking below the flung orlu of Mr. PilgrimWay, which came so close that he felt its wind and hate. Then Mr. Pilgrim-Way drew his limnae from behind his back, and with a wave of his hand, he burst the basement door open behind him, and they were in the first grade hall, and Mr. PilgrimWay, with another wave of his hand, burst that door open, and the snow began to come in, white and thick. He rushed out into it, and Ealgar followed, hacking, hacking.

Tommy Pepper screamed at Alice and Sullivan and

Belknap—"Get them out of there!"—and went after Ealgar and Mr. PilgrimWay.

He made sure he was holding his gyldn correctly.

The snow coming in from over the ocean was now blizzarding into a white blindness, and Tommy found Ealgar and Mr. PilgrimWay by the Plymouth Rock pavilion only by the sound of orlu on limnae. He ran after them and tried desperately to join the battle, but Ouslim the Liar moved so quickly, and so surely, that he kept Ealgar between them, and though Ealgar's play was swift and great, so too was that of Ouslim, and Ealgar began to tire under the onslaught.

His right arm grew heavy. His orlu dropped.

And immediately Ouslim the Liar swung the limnae into Ealgar's guts and Tommy heard the breath go out of him, and as he fell, Mr. PilgrimWay threw his knee against Ealgar's face and snapped his head back into unconsciousness.

And he turned to Tommy.

He twirled the limnae in his hand.

"You don't know how to hold that either, do you?" he said.

Then, as the snow flew wildly, Tommy was upon him.

Mr. PilgrimWay was startled—a gyldn against a limnae?—and he almost fell.

But he didn't.

He balanced himself against the pillars of the pavilion, took the limnae with both hands, and struck. And struck. And struck with hate.

Tommy kept the gyldn level against the blows, but each one beat against his arms and almost knocked him down.

He fled to the beach.

Now the wind was a shriek, and the snow avalanched so fast against him that he could barely see Mr. Pilgrim-Way or the beating limnae.

He was hardly surprised when the limnae smashed the gyldn from his hand.

He fell back onto the snowy sand.

"Now is the end of all things, Tommy Pepper," said Mr. PilgrimWay. Tommy could see the limnae quivering above him.

And then, he saw the open arms of the O'Mondim.

Whose two hands seemed to come right out of the blinding snow. They grasped Ouslim the Liar as with ykrat bands.

"Fah falettel," cried Mr. PilgrimWay. "Mondim fah falettel!"

Tommy stood, and there, suddenly, was Ealgar beside him, who held his orlu as one who could hardly bear its weight. He was breathing as if there were not enough air in this world. But he was also watching the O'Mondim, watching as if he could not believe what it was he saw.

And as Ouslim struggled wildly, yowling into the blizzard air, the O'Mondim turned his crumbling face to Tommy, and Tommy and Ealgar heard him speak: "Eac naman Pepper."

Ouslim slashed at the O'Mondim with the limnae, but the O'Mondim held him, and he turned and headed into the green waves, dragging the helpless Ouslim, who slashed at him again with the limnae, slashed again and again and again, shedding sand each time. But the O'Mondim did not stop. He dragged Ouslim into the white waves, past their breaking and into the depths, until with a final, horrible howl, they both went under, and the tormented water cascaded upward, and then again, and again, thrashed by the shrieking wind.

Ouslim the Liar was gone.

Immediately the wind dropped. The blizzard softened to easy, white flakes. Over the ocean, the sun came out and shone through the snow, turning the flakes gold.

Ealgar reached out his palm to catch them.

Tommy Pepper looked back toward William Bradford Elementary School, which glowed in the new sunlight. Everyone had come out—James Sullivan, and Patrick Belknap, and Alice Winslow holding Patty's hand, and even Mr. Burroughs, who couldn't quite stop yawning, and who was holding on to Patrick Belknap's shoulder in case he might topple over into another nap right there in the falling snow. And his father.

Tommy dropped his gyldn and held out his arms.

And Patty, Patty, Patty came running to him, crying, smiling.

Tommy looked at her, crying, smiling, too.

Tommy held her close, so close.

And suddenly, out in the water, there was a terrible thrashing, and dark water spewed up into the air, so high, so high, and where it fell, the water churned and churned, and the waves that had begun to pound the shore came well up onto the sand, and Tommy and Patty had to run back out of their way.

"Eteth threafta!" cried Ealgar.

"Keep out of the water!" called Tommy. "Belknap, get Mr. Burroughs back. Belknap! Keep out of the water!"

They ran away from the waves, the churning water following, obliterating the snow, foaming, stinking of rotten seaweed, boiling.

Then the pounding waves stilled.

The ocean fell calm.

And even as the snow stopped entirely, the sunshine spread quickly and surely over everything.

And illil it was. But Tommim Pepper and Ealgar the Bold and Alice Winslow and James Sullivan and Patrick Belknap—gumena weardas!—did stand on the shore and look out to the sea, where under the waves, the O'Mondim—eac naman Pepper—was already only the sand from which he had been made. And they bowed their heads, and Tommim Pepper wept for loss, all loss, and was not ashamed that he bawled like a first-grader.

That night, just before sunrise, Tommy Pepper and Patty and his father and Ealgar the Bold stood on the dune below their house.

Tommy held his chain.

He felt its heat, and into his mind came the bright hanorah playing on the days of the new year, of Hnaef and Hengest rising over green hills, of First Sunset over Langleth, of the flight of the wegelas—so many they darkened the skies with their white feathers and filled the air with their sweet callings—all those things the O'Mondim had lost when their faces were turned to the Silence.

But there were other pictures too. Pictures of picnics on the Plymouth shore, of climbs into the White Mountains on October days, of sitting atop the bronze ducklings of the Public Garden and his mother laughing laughing laughing at the faces that Tommy was making, of Patty only a few days old in her yellow crib, and of sitting beside his mother and playing the Bach piece with her—he could hear it—and it was at that picture that the chain glowed, even through Tommy Pepper's shirt.

Then did Ealgar the Bold, wrapped in a pea coat, stand before the three of them. Blithe he was, and glad for the downfall of Ouslim the Liar. Yet he did not know how the war at the Reced went, and in his heart, he grieved for what might befall the Ethelim. "Ne se weoruld," he said, and held out his hand.

Tommy Pepper nodded. But just for one more moment, he held the chain close to his heart and felt its heat. Just for one more moment, just for one more moment the lovely light of Hnaef, the warm heat of Hengest. Just for one more moment, the sound of his mother's voice, the brush of her hand on his hair, the . . .

No more. Tommy drew the chain over his head and held it out—he felt it all begin to leave him—and he placed the chain in the palm of Ealgar. And when he let it go, he could no longer even remember that there was something he had forgotten.

Except to know that part of him was gone. Again.

Ealgar took the chain and placed it around his neck, and he bowed to the Peppers.

"Tommim Pepper," he said. "Mod gethrief. Ethelim gethanc ond se gethanc. Mod strang, heort strang, mod strang."

Tommy Pepper did not understand a single word of what Ealgar said.

Ealgar smiled, nodded, and bowed again. He touched Tommy Pepper's chest—still warm where the chain had once been and was no more. Then Ealgar the Bold pressed the chain against his own chest, and a bright green burst threw itself against the golden light, on top of the fading blue. And Tommy Pepper and Patty and their father watched the bright burst rise, and rise and rise away, until the clouds bundled themselves together, and the light gave way, and the snow came down again, lightly, sweetly, beautifully.

For a long, long time, Tommy Pepper stood on the dune lit by the snow around him, and the tears were still on his face, and Patty reached and wiped at them, and Tommy knelt and held her tightly.

It snowed again that night, and then again the next day, and the next, so that Mr. Zwerger ended up calling the whole week off for snow days. But it was so bitterly cold that no one could go out, and by the beginning of the next week, everyone was almost happy to get back to William Bradford Elementary School because they'd been cooped up in their houses for so long.

Mr. Burroughs was glad to be back too. He couldn't quite understand how the days had gone by so quickly. Here it was almost Christmas break and they still hadn't finished their study on the solar system. They had a lot of work to do. And did anyone know what had happened to his Boston Red Sox posters?

There were others with lots of work to do too.

Cheryl Lumpkin decided that she wanted to take up the accordion. She and Patrick Belknap started to practice together during lunch recess until finally everyone in the class—even Mr. Burroughs—begged them to take their accordions down to the auditorium, where didn't they think the acoustics would be much better?

James Sullivan did get another football, and he decided not to try to get it signed by Tom Brady. He hadn't had much luck with Tom Brady–signed footballs. During recess—since Tommy would always go to practice piano— he threw with Alice Winslow, who turned out to have a really good arm herself, and who every so often made a catch that even Pepper would have applauded, if he'd been there.

Mr. Zwerger gave up painting, since he couldn't figure out how to make the figures move. He was sure that once a long time ago someone had shown him how to do that, but now . . . Well, perhaps he would put it all away for a while and try again another time. He gave all the art supplies to Mrs. MacReady, who put them in a box and carried them down to the basement, even though she wasn't paid to do that.

Mrs. Lumpkin had had enough of trampled and missing yellow flags by the Pepper house, never mind the madman that lived in the neighborhood. So she gave up her Pilgrim Way Condominium project after all. She found a much better location in East Sandwich, and the owner agreed to swap the land for a top-floor condo and a yellow Mazda as long as those scratches were repaired.

Everyone was pleased, and when the condominiums were built, Mrs. Lumpkin hung her portrait—which Mrs. MacReady found in the basement of the school—in the lobby.

And she did, finally, pay for it.

Tommy Pepper put his gyldn above the door to his room. Most nights he would take it down and try to figure out how to hold it correctly. He thought he should remember what it had once been for, but he didn't. And he couldn't understand why his Ace Robotroid Adventure lunch box reminded him of something . . . something he couldn't figure out exactly. There was Ace Robotroid flying through the skies in his red cape. What else would anyone expect on an Ace Robotroid Adventure lunch box?

He couldn't see the pictures of his mother in the pale yellow of the hall anymore either, but somehow he remembered her more sharply than he had for a long time. Every memory brought, now, a smile. And on cold nights, when the snow was blowing outside and the fireplace glowing inside, Tommy sat down at the piano—his father watched him from the kitchen, where he was tearing up the old linoleum—and he set his fingers over the keys and felt heat in them. Real heat. Where did it come from?

And he played.

The Bach piece.

And Patty would come and sit beside him, until one

night, Tommy realized she was humming. Really. Her head lay against his shoulder, and she was humming.

Their notes came sweetly. They filled the room and their hearts. They filled the whole house, until they sounded outside and floated down to the shore and then lifted themselves upward, toward the lighted stars.

TWENTY-ONE

The New Days of the Ethelim

*W*hen Young Waeglim woke, he felt hands against *his shoulder that stilled the blood and gentled the hurt of his wounds. A dark coat lay over him, and beside him knelt Ealgar the Bold.*

And around the neck of Ealgar the Bold was the Art of the Valorim, glowing in the red light of Second Sunset. Then did Ealgar help Young Waeglim to stand, and they came through the shattered doors of the Tower Room and down the stairs of the Tower of the Reced, through the ruined room of the Seats of the Reced and down into the Great Hall and the Courts of the Ethelim, where the battle had stilled, as if there was no more to fight for, and none to fight with.

Then did Ealgar the Bold hold his hand high above his head, and the gleaming brightness that came from it was the light of the Art of the Valorim, and it shone

over them all, so that the O'Mondim host and the Ethelim of the Reced were amazed, and they did drop their
tools of war. The hanoraho sounded—though none
knew how—and a great cry went up from the Ethelim
of the Reced, for Ealgar had returned.

Then, as all in the Courts of the Ethelim watched,
Ealgar the Bold bowed before the last of the Valorim,
and Ealgar held the Art of the Valorim out to Young
Waeglim, but he denied it, and would not take it. And
when Ealgar the Bold pressed it upon him, and when
the Ethelim called his name, then did Young Waeglim
finally take the chain, but he held it aloft, and he laid it
around the neck of Ealgar the Bold.

Another cry went up, and another, and then
did Ealgar come to the O'Mondim host, and with the
Art of the Valorim he touched the forehead of each
of the O'Mondim, and their eyes and mouths were
opened, and their hearts beat again, and they knew who
they were.

It is a story told over and over again: How Ealgar
told the O'Mondim the tale of an O'Mondim in a far-
away world who had given all for his people, whom he
had never seen, and how he had saved them, and how
his name was Pepper, and how the O'Mondim then did
dance under the tuning stars that night, lit by the last of
the bursting naeli of ancient Ecglaef.

It is a story told over and over again: How the

*Ethelim of the Reced did dance with the O'Mondim,
and were filled with a joy beyond what they could ever
have hoped, and how none were gladder than Bruleath,
and Hileath, his daughter, and Ealgar, his son.*

*It is a story told over and over again: How long
before First Sunrise, the O'Mondim removed from
the Courts of the Reced, and did leave that country for
their own.*

*It is a story told over and over again: How Young
Waeglim the Noble did rest from his grievous wounds
that night, but after Second Sunrise, he had gone to
those places where none can follow, and the wuduo
were hung for forty-eight days, and the mourning was
great for the last of the Valorim, who had borne so
much for the Ethelim of the Reced.*

*It is a story told over and over again: How Ealgar
the Bold, Guardian of the Art of the Valorim, Gumena
Weardas, did reign with his father and his sister among
the Twelve Sovereigns of the Reced, and brought new
peace to his world. Ever he was among the people of
the Reced, and ever did his heart move to theirs, and
it was said that he, and he alone, knew where the
country of the O'Mondim was, and that he was wel-
comed there.*

*But most nights, Ealgar would climb to the Tower
Room of the Reced, and step through a shattered door
that was never repaired. And by the window, beside a*

ruined Forge, he would listen to strange music. Music that came from far away. Sweet music from among the lighted stars.

The Testament of Young Waeglim

Written in the House of Bruleath of the Ethelim
in the City of the Ethelim

Year 1058 since the Coming of the Valorim
into This World

Tomorrow's battle will be my last. Afterward, there may be nothing but Silence. Yet afterward, there may be a new world, where the Ethelim shall come into their full destiny as a people, and the long work of the Valorim be triumphant. Either way, the days of the Valorim in this world are over. So I write this last Testament of the Valorim, that their ancient purposes may be remembered.

Well more than ten centuries ago—centuries as measured here—the Valorim did come to this world to find a people in despair. These were the Ethelim, those who had survived the Great Burning, when the two suns that lit their world came close in an orbit that was one in ten thousand of their centuries, and so destroyed everything but a remnant of their people. This coming together had been predicted by Ecglaeth of the Valorim, and it was Ecglaeth who brought the first Valorim to this world to see if any had survived. They found but few. None of the cities was aught but waste and ashes. None of the towns was aught but stains against a burned landscape.

Then did Ecglaeth together with Elder Waeglim and Hengel and Hengaelf and the gentle Elil gather the Ethelim together and bring them under the shadow of the mountains of the Valley of Denvelf, below the Plains of Arnulf, where the land was watered by the snow off the mountains, and the land, though burned, was rich beneath the surface. And there they founded the City of the Ethelim. And on the Plain of Benu, Hengaelf planted the Long Woods—which the Ethelim gave to him for his own from where the Valley of Denvelf flattens toward Sorg Cynnes to where the shadow of Langleth reaches at dawn. And together the Valorim and Ethelim planted and watered the lands below and around the new city, and so the Ethelim were saved.

But none of this was done with ease, and to help the Ethelim, Hengel and the gentle Elil did journey above the Falls of Hagor, and there, beneath the sea, in a place that none but they knew, they used the Art of the Valorim to bring life to the O'Mondim, children of the watery sands of this world, who opened their eyes, saw the bright stars, and did sing for the beauty they knew. They traveled over the mountains past Tillil, and when they came above the Plains of Arnulf, they did plant great trees that grow there still. And so they came down across the Plains, and to the City of the Ethelim, where they built the Reced of that city, and its walls and streets, side by side with the Ethelim. And at night, the O'Mondim sang songs to the stars, songs that swelled like the waves they were born in.

When the Reced was finished, the Twelve Seats of the Ethelim were set in their chamber so that the Ethelim might rule over their city. And in a Tower high above them, the Forge of the Valorim was built, and fired, and it was the seat of the Valorim Art, where matter and song were hammered together into a power that protected and nurtured all that world. And when these were built and the City of the Ethelim was shining fair under the Twin Suns, Ecglaef of the Valorim did sprinkle the night sky with bright lights, and the hanoraho sounded.

And so, for more than nine of this world's centuries, the City of the Ethelim was at peace. And the Long Woods of Benu grew green and tall, as did the O'Mondim woods above the Plains of Arnulf. And below the city, the gentle Elil did build homes for the Valorim in his hills, and there did Ecglaeth dwell, and Elder Waeglim, and Hild and his ten daughters, and Brythelaf with his sons, and many of the Valorim who did not dwell in Bawn, by Sorg Cynnes, near the Long Woods. But in Bawn did dwell Hengel and Hengaelf. And there too did dwell Hrunlaeth, who would not make a home near the Ethelim.

And it was in Bawn that Hrunlaeth deceived Hengaelf, who traded the Long Woods of Benu for an orlu of worthless metal. So the idea came to Hrunlaeth that if he could gain one part of the world of the Ethelim so easily, *why not gain it all? Thus he became Mondus, and he first brought around him Saphim, and Ouslim, and Calorim, and Verlim, and Naelim, and Fralim, and Remlin, who were of like mind to Mondus. And in his deceptions, Mondus sent Naelim to the Hills of Elil with sweet words to treat with Ecglaeth, and to ask him to come to Bawn. But when Ecglaeth would not, for he suspected treachery, Naelim waited for Second Sunset, and killed him.*

It was the first murder among the Valorim. Treachery was opened.

Now did the brothers Belim and Belalim join with Mondus. Wanting the whole world for themselves, the faithless Valorim planned for battle at Sorg Cynnes— though they feared the numbers of the faithful Valorim, and the Ethelim who might rally with them. Thus did Mondus send Ouslim to the City of the Ethelim, to the O'Mondim, to sway them with false promises—but they would not be swayed.

Then did Fralim warp his Art, and gave his eyes to it, and with his Art, he did blind and smother all the faces of the O'Mondim, and Ouslim went again to them in their despair, and said to the O'Mondim that they had lost what they had lost because of the wrath of the faithful Valorim, who believed that they would betray them. Then did the O'Mondim march to the Hills of Elil and slaughter the gentle Elil. And they marched to Bawn, and in the Battle of Sorg Cynnes, they betrayed and slew Hengel, who had been at their birth past the Falls of Hagor. So did die the only two of the Valorim who knew where that place was.

But then did Elder Waeglim lead the Valorim out of the City of the Ethelim, together with a host of the Ethelim, and they did come upon Mondus at Sorg Cynnes, and there did they do great battle. And Elder Waeglim stood as iron on the field, but at First Sunset, he fell sorely wounded, and if it had not been for Bruleath of the Ethelim, he would have died that day on the field. But Bruleath stood by him at the battle surge, and he—an Ethelim—did rally the Valorim, and together they built the Wall of Ice around the fallen Elder Waeglim, and did repel the O'Mondim. By Second Sunset, the faithless Valorim and Mondus had fled into the Long Woods, together with the faceless O'Mondim. And Elder Waeglim still breathed. And he and Bruleath became brothers of the heart.

But Mondus was not fallen. He crossed through the Long Woods and up into the Valley of Denvelf, and then across the mountains to the Valley of Wyssiel, and there he bound the faceless O'Mondim to him, so that their only love was their hate for the Valorim, and their only trust was in Mondus. And for three winters Mondus grew strong.

Elder Waeglim returned to the City of the Ethelim, and he too grew strong, and he was often at the house of Bruleath of the Ethelim.

Then, together with Taeglim and Yolim, Elder Waeglim

built the battlements above the city at Brogum Sorg Cynna, for they suspected that Mondus would return with the O'Mondim. And Taeglim and Yolim built the battlements wondrous fair and wide and high, so that none might come into the city unless they were allowed to pass the battlements. But Elder Waeglim did not know, and could not have known, that it was his folly to trust Taeglim and Yolim, and that already they were tempted to turn to Mondus, who had seduced them.

And so, the army of Mondus gathered on the Plains of Arnulf, and those who stood on the battlements of Brogum Sorg Cynna looked out and beheld an endless sea of the faceless O'Mondim, and around them, the faithless Valorim, who stoked them with their hate, and who, with the rising of Hreth, drove them across the Plains to Brogum Sorg Cynna, and there they did meet the army of the Ethelim and the might of Elder Waeglim, who stood on the battlements with a hardened heart, for behind him, back in the city, Ferth was abed, tended by the daughters of Hild, for she was giving birth to a son.

And so wave after wave of the faceless O'Mondim broke upon the battlements of Brogum Sorg Cynna, and the Ethelim cheered to the echo from mighty Langleth.

Yet First Sunrise brought treachery with it.

When the light of First Sunrise fell upon the battlements by the Long Woods, the stones exploded. One by *one, they became dust and dust only—this through the terrible Art of Taeglim and Yolim—and the Ethelim and the Valorim who stood upon their ramparts fell to their ends. When Elder Waeglim turned to find Taeglim and Yolim, they were gone to their new lord, and nothing could stop the fall of the battlements of Brogum Sorg Cynna.*

Then did Elder Waeglim order all away from the falling battlements, and they formed lines before the City of the Ethelim, the Valorim together with the Ethelim, and they stood waiting for the faceless O'Mondim, who flowed over the fallen battlements like a flood, and thrust into the Ethelim and Valorim. The Valorim and Ethelim fell back again and again, until they reached the walls of the city itself. And there, Elder Waeglim did call to those around him, and urged them to the greatness they needed. "Now is the time for all to hold fast," he said. "Now is the time for strong arms, strong hearts, and strong spirits."

From that moment, the line did not falter, nor did it fall back. They stood as one, as iron, as powerful as the fallen battlements. And the O'Mondim could not come at them, and the O'Mondim fell into Silence.

It was in the heat of that battle that Young Waeglim was born and did breathe his first breath. And not long after, Elder Waeglim did breathe his last breath, so he never did see his son. But Mondus had fled again, and the O'Mondim host was defeated, and they returned to the Valley of Wyssiel. There they dwelled for eighteen years, while the Ethelim ruled their city from the Twelve Seats, and while Young Waeglim dwelled in the glory of his father and did come to learn the Art of the Valorim, until he was made the Master of the Forge, and did practice the Art in the heat of its fire.

For all those years, Mondus brooded in the Valley of Wyssiel, and brooded, and brooded, even as he gathered the faceless O'Mondim again. And the Valorim were foolish. They would not believe that Mondus would battle them a third time. They were wrong. When he was most ready, Mondus drove the O'Mondim through the Valley of Wyssiel, and below the Long Woods and below the Field of Sorg Cynnes and even below the Hills of Elil. And then, in a march impossible to imagine, he came by night to the City of the Ethelim, which had grown accustomed to nights of peace, and whose gates were wide.

The O'Mondim were in the city before any of the Valorim knew of it, and they were upon the Reced itself as fast as Thought. When they burst into the Reced, there was great battle, and the sons of Brythelaf fell, and the daughters of Hild, and the Twelve Seats were overthrown, and it was left to Young Waeglim to forge the Art of the Valorim into a single Chain so that it might be sent out of this world and not fall into the grip of Mondus—none knows now whether that sending was for good or for ill.

And in that battle by the Forge, Brythelaf fell, and Young Waeglim—whose hand writes this Testament—became the last of the faithful Valorim in this world.

Tomorrow, even he may be gone, and the O'Mondim may be triumphant.

All depends upon one last, most desperate chance.

A List of Weird and Strange Words
That Came Out of the Mouth of Tommy Pepper
and Which He Now Claims
He Never Said But He Did Say
Even If He Says He Didn't or Doesn't Remember He Did

With a Little Help from Mr. Burroughs

By Alice Winslow

ALDER: Wine. Tommy pretended he knew what he was talking about here, but he didn't.

ALORN: A planet in a galaxy far away. It has rings, sort of like Saturn, probably.

ARNULF: Plains to the north of the City of the Ethelim, except they don't use north, said Tommy. They use something to do with the position of their twin suns. I don't think he understood this very well.

BELOIT: Art of all types. Maybe.

BENU: A deep and dark woods, named after something older than the Valorim. No one knows what the word means. See *Denvelf.*

BROGUM: Wall or battlements or barrier or barricade or something like that. It's meant to stand against a siege or an attack.

BYRGUM BARUT: This seems to be a curse. Tommy would not translate it for me, but the way he said it made things seem pretty clear. When he really wanted to say it like a curse, he added *Su*. So it went *Su byrgum barut*. Sure sounds like a curse to me.

CYNNA: Field of tall grasses.

DENVELF: A valley named for something older than the Valorim, but no one knows what the word means. The valley is known for its fruit—don't ask me what kind.

DUR: Cold.

EAC: Also.

ECGLAEF: The inventor of *naeli*. See *naeli*.

ETETH THREAFTA: These two words seem to go together. They mean "Stay out of the water." I think *threafta* means "water." But maybe *eteth* does.

ETHELIM: The name of a group of people.

ETHELRAD: The main road in a city. I am guessing that *rad* means "road," which, when you think of it, is really close to English.

FAH: Really dirty or ugly or smelly or disgusting. Like Cheryl Lynn Lumpkin.

FALETTEL: This is a curse that Tommy used because Mr. Burroughs would take him down to the main office if he used words that he shouldn't and Mr. Burroughs didn't know this was a curse so Tommy figured he could use it.

FERR: To make or to create. Or to do something.

GLITE: Glass or windows.

GLITELOIT: Art made from glass or maybe art made from light itself—but that is hard to imagine.

GUMENA WEARDAS: I think these words go together and mean "brave people" or "brave warriors." Or it might mean "brave warrior," so one warrior or several. It is definitely a compliment, and despite what James Sullivan said, it is not meant to refer to boys only. James Sullivan can be such a jerk sometimes.

GYLDN: A weapon like a dagger. It is worn at the belt.

HALIN: A weapon that seems like a short sword. I don't think Tommy knew how to use one. Or how to even hold one.

HANORAH: This one is from Mr. Burroughs. He thinks that it is an instrument—sort of like a French horn but much bigger—that is blown at special occasions. He said that the plural is *hanoraho*, which sort of sounds like someone is trying to yodel but isn't very good at it.

HARNEUF: One of the Valorim, who cut spectacular jewels.

HENGAELF: One of the Valorim, who owned the Woods of Benu but who apparently wasn't the cleverest of them all since he lost the woods in some sort of stupid deal.

HENGEST: A name for the sun.

HNAEF: Another name for the sun. This is confusing. It sounds like Tommy meant that this is the sun that rises first in the morning and sets first in the evening, and that Hengest is the sun that rises second and sets second. This would mean that there are two different suns, I guess.

HRETH: A name for the moon.

HRUNTUM: Temporary houses built by a shore. These are washed away twice a year by the highest *rylim* tides—which goes to show why they were temporary. See *rylim tides.*

ILLIL: Beautiful or lovely.

KARFYER: One of the Valorim, who was an artist. He always left one part of his work of art unfinished.

LIMNAE: This is another weapon—as if Tommy needed another weapon. It is long and like a whip of metal and is worn across the back. Tommy said he knew how to handle this but I don't think he really did.

MAEGLIA: Weak, helpless, or useless. Tommy sometimes used this as an adjective, like "Jeremy Hereford is *maeglia*." But sometimes he used it like a noun, like "He is a *maeglia*." Either he didn't know which was which, or it can work both ways.

MELUS: A sweet drink made with something like honey. Tommy said it was like grape juice but a completely different flavor. This isn't a very helpful description.

MOD: When I asked him what this meant, Tommy pointed to his stomach and said, "Guts." I don't know if he meant bravery or his intestines.

NAELI: Fireworks.

NANIG: Not any. I'm not sure if this was really a word in this language or if Tommy was just saying it funny.

NEFER: Never. This is probably another word that Tommy was just saying funny. Sometimes he doesn't know when to stop. He liked to say it when Patrick Belknap was reaching for his accordion.

NUNC GLAEDRE NON: I think this is a saying. It means something like, "Never again will there be happiness" or "You won't be seeing good times around here anymore." This is a depressing language.

NYSSI: Tommy used this to describe a kind of order—so, "in order of *nyssi*." I never could figure out what this order was. I think it had something to do with color, but I'm not sure.

O'MONDIM: The name of a group of monsters. At least, I think they are monsters. Maybe not.

ORLU: A weapon that you wear at your shoulder. The plural is *orluo*, so I guess adding an *o* in this language is like our adding an *s*. I don't think Tommy knew how to hold this weapon either.

RAU: A boat. Tommy never said what kind, but it sounds like a boat with a sail.

RECED: A castle. Tommy said that it was built for the Ethelim by the Valorim.

RUCCA: Dirty or ugly or smelly or disgusting. Plymouth Harbor on a really bad day. Or the basement of William Bradford Elementary any day.

RYLIM TIDES: The highest tides that come only twice a year and destroy the *hruntum*. See *hruntum*.

SELITH: Relax.

SLYTHING: A sneaky walk, used by the O'Mondim and sometimes Mr. Zwerger in order to catch someone.

SORG: I think this is a certain kind of stone that is very hard and heavy. I asked Tommy if it was like Plymouth Rock, and he said it was a lot harder and heavier than Plymouth Rock, but how would he know that?

STRANG: I guessed "strange" but Tommy gave me a look that said I was an idiot and he said it means "strong." Then I said it should probably mean "strangle," and Mr. Burroughs told us to stop.

SYN: After.

THRIMBLE: A technique used in painting—and maybe other arts, but in painting for sure. In this technique, the artist makes things on the canvas move—not appear to move, but really move. Like a goat chewing grass, say.

THRYGETH: The very, very last completed part of a work of art that gives it its power.

TOMBRADISIND: No idea what this means, but it seems important to Tommy. James Sullivan also uses this word. I think it means that something is good. Like, say, "Mr. Burroughs is a *tombradisind* teacher." I think.

TREMPE: A loud drum. The plural is *trempo*.

TRUNC: Another weapon, this one used by the O'Mondim. It is made out of a gray metal. Its plural is *trunco*.

UNFERE: Not beautiful, but not horribly ugly. Somewhere in between, but tending toward the ugly side of things. Sort of like Mrs. MacReady.

VALORIM: The name of another group of people.

VITRIE: A predator that sounds like some sort of reptile, like a dragon. It has talons that sink into you—which sounds very drag-ony. The plural is *vitrio*.

WEGELAS: White birds, sort of like seagulls, but smaller.

WEORULD: Globe or world or planet. Or this could be another word that Tommy was just saying funny.

WUDUO: Long banners that are usually black. They are hung on high walls when someone important has died. Like a president, I guess.

YKRAT: This sounds like a rope made out of something like iron. It is very strong and cannot be broken. I said it could probably also mean "love" and Tommy didn't say no.